BUYER

Hi!

I think it's only fair to warn you. Most of the words in this book are pretty harmless. Like the word 'harmless', for example. Or 'example'. Or 'or'. However (another example), there are a few that you wouldn't want to shout out in church or in front of your dear old silver-haired granny. Well, I'm assuming you wouldn't.

Let me be a bit more specific. On four occasions I use a word that if you yelled it in Maths class would probably get you suspended. Another word, used eleven times, might get you a lunchtime detention. Finally, a word used fourteen times would result in the kind of ticking off that invariably starts, 'I'm very disappointed in you, young lady/man [delete as appropriate] ...'

Twenty-nine words. Or 0.04% of all the words in the book. Statistically insignificant, as my Maths teacher would say. And he should know. He's built his entire teaching career around insignificance, but that's another story. Anyway, just thought you should know.

Try it. Read page 129

BARRY JONSBERG was born in England but now lives and works in Darwin, Australia where he has discovered that the sky is actually blue, not grey as he had always believed. He teaches English at a local high school, but his students rarely let that get in the way of having a good time in his classes. When he is not teaching or writing, his wife Anita takes him for a walk on the beach, though he mistakenly believes that this is for the benefit of their two dogs. He loves watching his favourite soccer team, Liverpool, on the TV and labours under the delusion that the English cricket team is on the brink of giving Australia a good game. Apart from that, he is pretty much in contact with the real world.

the whole business with kiffo and the pit bull

Barry Jonsberg

EGMONT

EGMONT

We bring stories to life

First published in Australia 2004 by Allen & Unwin
Published in Great Britain 2005
by Egmont Books Limited
239 Kensington High Street, London W8 6SA

Text copyright © 2004 Barry Jonsberg
Cover illustration copyright © 2004 Oliver Burston
Converse Chuck Taylor All-Star shoe image used with the
permission of Converse Inc.

ISBN 1 4052 1767 7

1 3 5 7 9 10 8 6 4 2

A CIP catalogue record for this title is available from the British Library

Typeset by Avon DataSet Ltd, Bidford on Avon
Printed and bound in Great Britain by the CPI Group

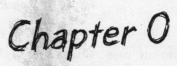

Chapter 0

ASSIGNMENT:

Write a description of a place, person or thing in such a way that you demonstrate an understanding of the use of similes.

RESPONSE:

Student's name: Calma Harrison

Subject: Jaryd Kiffing

Kiffo's hair is like a glowing sunset. However, unlike a sunset, it lasts for a long time and doesn't suddenly turn black and become studded with stars. It is as wild as a dingo on drugs and sticks up like ears of corn after a cyclone. Maybe like a field of corn that is the colour of sunset, and has been trampled by a whole load of drug-crazed dingoes during a cyclone.

Kiffo's nose is like butter on toast. It was put on hot and it spread. His nostrils gape like two huge caves, but it would be difficult to camp in them or even light a fire in them. Though it might be worth trying, I suppose. They drip like your swimsuit when you hang it over the pool railings to dry. His eyes are as brown as diarrhoea, which only goes to prove that he is full of crap. Kiffo's teeth are like stars because they come out at night. No, that's just an old joke. His teeth are as white as sheets that were once white but have now become stained by unmentionable things. Kiffo's neck is short and dirty, like life. His arms are as thin as pencils, but if you try to sharpen them he'll probably bash you. His legs are bent like brackets ( ), but unlike brackets there is not much of interest between them. When he stands he is like a cowboy who hasn't realised that the horse he was riding has gone for a ciggie break. He smells like a fish that you forgot was in the fridge.

His mind is as shallow as a gob of spit in a drained swimming pool. Kiffo is as intellectually challenging as a meeting of English teachers.

So. What do you think? Be honest. I mean, it's not as if we know each other, so you can say what you like and I'm not going to be offended. It would be different, I suppose, if we hung out together at the local mall, or invited each other for sleep-overs, or you had my name tattooed on your left buttock. Your judgement would be clouded. There was a study done. I can't remember where, but I think it might have been in America. A psychologist compared students' class work with their appearance and a direct correlation was found between physical attractiveness and grades. In other words, if you look like Brad Pitt or J.Lo then you are more likely to get an A than someone who looks like the rear end of a lower primate. Interesting, huh? I think there are three possible judgements, based on this research, we can make about teachers:

1. Teachers are, like the rest of humanity, flawed, and we should understand that they are subject to the same frailties as everyone else.
2. Teachers are superficial idiots.
3. Teachers are both of the above.

But if I've learned one thing over the last month or so, it's that judgements are very dangerous things.

Anyway, have you made your objective assessment of the simile exercise? Good. Hold that thought.

END OF TERM REPORT:

Student's name:	Calma Harrison
Teacher:	Ms Brinkin
Subject:	English
Grade:	A-
Attitude:	C-

<u>Comments:</u>

Calma is an exceptionally talented student of English. Unfortunately, she seems determined to waste her considerable ability. She needs to understand that assignments must be taken seriously, and are not merely an opportunity to display her quirky and, at times, immature sense of humour. I expect a marked improvement in her attitude next semester.

Teacher's name:	Ms Brinkin
Student:	Calma Harrison
Subject:	English
Grade:	D–
Attitude:	C–

Comments:

Ms Brinkin has a considerable talent for mediocrity and she seems determined to reach her full potential in this area. Her assignments are of an antiquity that would fascinate educational historians and she is justifiably proud of never having entertained an original idea. Her lessons are delivered in a whining monotone that only occasionally threatens to disturb the class's established sleeping patterns. An enormous improvement on last semester. Well done!

Chapter 1

Kiffo's finest moment

Imagine the scene. There is a new English teacher in the school, replacing the unlamented Ms Brinkin who has disappeared interstate. Rumour has it that 'Stinkin' Brinkin' left in pursuit of her personal goal to stunt the educational development of as many young Australians as she can find. A woman with a mission and, if past experience is anything to go by, every chance of succeeding.

The new teacher is young and inexperienced. She thinks

that she can get through to the kids, bless her. That she can make a difference, mould minds, instil a love of literature into the lumpy heads of Kiffo and the other dazzlingly dysfunctional dumbbells that make up my Year 10 English class. She is frighteningly cheerful, smiling at everyone all the time and generally spooking us out. She over-prepares her lessons. You can tell that she spends hours and hours at home developing materials that she thinks are interesting. In short, she's a disaster waiting to happen.

I love it when we get a teacher like that. What will happen? When will she decide that it's too much effort, that those hours are a waste, that she could have spent the time more profitably getting drunk, or sleeping, or watching TV? When will she come in with defeat stamped on her face and give us an exercise taken from a book that is twenty years old? When will she stop marking our assignments with detailed comments and just put big ticks at the bottom of every unread page? How long will she struggle against the inevitable?

Miss Leanyer. She was great while she lasted. Of course, most of the class didn't really give a stuff. Generally speaking we did what we were told to do, because . . . well, that's just the way it was. We didn't have the energy or the interest to keep up a battle. That's not to say that we were saints. Oh, no. We did all the normal stuff: doodling on each other's legs in black felt tip, dismantling the furniture with nailfiles, talking while Miss Leanyer was trying to explain the mating habits of apostrophes. That kind of thing.

But Kiffo . . . mad, magnificent Kiffo . . . well, he saw matters differently. For him, a teacher, particularly a new teacher, had no rights at all. They weren't human, really. For Kiffo, it was nothing less than his solemn duty to give them a hard time.

So there he was, sitting at the back of the class, idly tossing a footy in the air. Feet up on the desk. No books out, of course. Miss Leanyer was trying to get us to read a short story about teenage love written by someone who was, quite clearly, 120 years old. To be fair to her, she knew enough not to ask Kiffo to read out loud. He didn't do that. Ever. And he had made it plain that no one should ever ask him to. Nonetheless, the footy was really distracting, which is just what Kiffo intended. After ten minutes, Miss Leanyer couldn't ignore it any more.

'Jaryd,' she said. The infinite patience in her voice made you want to poke her in the eye with a sharpened stick. 'Put the ball away, please.'

'In a minute, Miss,' replied Kiffo, throwing the ball from one hand to the other.

'Not in a minute, Jaryd. Now, please.'

Kiffo's mouth twitched slightly. Not quite a smile, but I knew the signs. He had her hooked. It was just a question of reeling her in now, enjoying the battle. He tossed the ball into the air again. I looked from one to the other, like I was the ball girl in a tennis match. You know, when the ball is whipping across the net and you risk whiplash to keep it in vision. Kiffo seeded number one; Miss Leanyer a wild card. Outgunned. Wow, I'm mixing my metaphors, but you know what I mean. So there's this silence for about ten seconds. A challenge thrown down. It was much better than the short story we were reading. Miss Leanyer moved slightly, her eyes darting down to her desk. I knew what was going through her mind. She'd issued an order. Probably regretted it now, but it was too late. She had to see it through to its conclusion. She cleared her throat.

'If you don't put the ball away now, Jaryd, I'll confiscate it.'

'You can't do that, Miss. It's my property and you don't have no right to take what belongs to me.'

Standard stuff, so far. We all knew the 'it's my property' routine. Not that we had any idea if it was true or not. But it seemed to work most times. That's the thing with people like Kiffo. He knew his rights. Or thought he did. Classroom lawyers, one and all. I looked again at Miss Leanyer. 'Your move,' I thought.

'Get your feet off the desk,' she said. 'Now!'

No 'please' this time. I love that about teachers. They all have this in-built politeness even when they are dealing with vermin. 'I would like you to take that knife away from the Principal's throat and stop setting the school on fire, please.' Always the 'please'. Maybe they think that it will somehow seep into the student's unconscious mind. Role models of politeness. But this was getting interesting. She had covered his bet and upped the ante by sticking another five hundred dollars on top. I could see them in an old Western, facing each other across a cheap table in the local saloon. There'd be a tired honky-tonk pianist in the background and a bartender, with rolled-up sleeves, skimming slugs of whisky across a polished surface to dusty cowboys.

'I think you're bluffing, Mister, and I'm prepared to put my money on it.' The piano would pause and painted women would stop toying with their frilly garters.

I was riveted.

Kiffo slowly moved one foot off the table. He sat there, one hairy leg stuck on the side of the desk, tilting back in his chair. If you looked carefully, you could see up his shorts. Enough to make a girl gag. The ball spun slowly on Kiffo's hand.

'Both feet off the desk and stop leaning back on your chair. This instant!'

What? Two things to do at the same time? Doesn't compute. Neurones burning out, smoke coming from the ears. Fantastic. I hadn't had such fun in ages. Miss Leanyer was really going for it. The whole class was absorbed, praying that the bell wouldn't go until this little drama had been played out to its conclusion. Comedy or tragedy? It could go either way.

'Unless you do as you're told now, you will leave this classroom.'

As you have probably gathered, I'm something of an

expert in these matters. An acute observer of classroom relationships. And you're probably wondering about my reaction to this last statement. Well, there's a couple of things to be said about it. Firstly, Miss Leanyer had done well by not threatening detention. Kiffo would have laughed in her face. He didn't do detention. He knew well enough that the school needed a parent's written permission to keep you behind after normal school hours. He also knew that his parent would never give permission. So detention was a completely idle threat. But the notion of sending him out of the room was fatally flawed as well. She'd left herself with no room to back out. No path of retreat. They should teach that in whatever places teach teachers how to be teachers. Sorry, bit clumsy. But you get my point. If Kiffo said, 'Get stuffed', then how was she to force him? She couldn't touch him. We all knew *those* rights! Mind you, I doubt if she would have wanted to touch him.

Secondly, what kind of a threat was it? 'I'll send you out.' Oh, horrors. Unthinkable. Do you really mean, Miss, that I'll have to forgo the rest of this really crappy short story? Enough to make the strongest man blanch. I don't think so.

Anyway, it turned out OK. In the short term, at least. Kiffo slowly swung his other foot off the desk. Of course, it wasn't really two orders after all. With both feet off the desk, he couldn't keep leaning back in his chair. And that's where it should have ended. I mean, Miss Leanyer had done better than anyone could have hoped. She had got him to obey an instruction. Flushed with success, however, she pushed it too far. Think of it this way. If you had just stuck both your feet into a crocodile-infested river and dangled them around for five minutes, you'd be happy to still have them attached to your legs, wouldn't you? You wouldn't think that it was a good idea to put your head in as an encore. But that's what Miss Leanyer did. I couldn't believe it.

'Now get your books out and put that football away, Jaryd Kiffing.'

She turned back to the blackboard without waiting for a response. Maybe that was her big mistake. I'm not sure. All I know is that Kiffo twirled the ball on his index finger and, with a quick sidelong glance at the rest of the class, launched it into the air. I watched in fascination as the ball left Kiffo's hand. It arced slowly over the desks. I knew, I swear to God I knew, that his aim was perfect. Think of all those films where the real action happens in slow motion. Miss Leanyer, her head turned away from the class, moving slowly, oh so slowly towards the board. A piece of chalk resting leisurely in her hand. The ball reaching the highest point of its flight, turning gradually in the tension-ridden air. Students swivelling their heads to watch. It took ages. It was as if the ball was attached to the back of Miss Leanyer's head by a piece of strong, invisible elastic. I'm even prepared to swear that at one stage she moved her head upwards *and the ball adjusted its flight path,* like one of those heat-seeking missiles.

It hit her smack on the back of the head.

That would have been bad enough, but her face was so close to the blackboard that the force shoved her head forward so that she head-butted the board. It was a hell of a whack. I nearly wet myself with excitement. I mean, I'm not a sadist or anything. I still think it was really sad, what Kiffo did to her. But you had to be there to appreciate it. It was . . . thrilling.

Miss Leanyer turned towards the class. I might have been the first to see it – that mad look in her eyes, like someone who has been really close to an edge and then suddenly gets a shove that puts them right over. I can't swear to it, obviously. Maybe even then she would have kept control. Difficult to say. But if you want my opinion, it was Kiffo's smirk and his comment – 'Sorry, Miss, it slipped' – that really did the damage. What happened next was all a bit confusing. Before we knew it, Miss Leanyer – that small, quiet, timid teacher – had turned into a raving lunatic. She jumped across the desks, clearing students' heads by a good margin, and fell on Kiffo like an avenging harpy. Face twisted into a mad grimace, she had him by the throat and was banging his head against the wall.

It was the look on Kiffo's face that was the best of all. He was completely taken by surprise. I mean, who wouldn't be? And his look was saying, 'This can't be happening to me', as Miss Leanyer's fingers tightened around his throat. She was growling, like an enraged animal. Spit flecked her face. I believe that she would have killed him if someone hadn't intervened. We didn't, of course. Stunned, I guess. But the door crashed open and Mr Brewer, the teacher from next door, flew into the room. I imagine he was coming in to complain about some kid banging on the partition wall while he was trying to teach. But he took one look at the situation and leaped into action.

The last we ever saw of Miss Leanyer, she was being dragged by Mr Brewer out of the classroom door, her eyes mad with rage, fingers clawing the air for Kiffo's throat. A pity really. I reckon she would have had our attention and respect for the rest of the term. Even Kiffo might have got his books out for her. He wouldn't have written in them, of course. I'm not that much of a romantic.

So that was that. We never found out what happened to Miss Leanyer. There were rumours, naturally. Some said that she had given up teaching and had taken to mud wrestling down south for a living. If her attack on Kiffo was anything to go by, she would have been good at it too. Others said that she was a stripper in Kings Cross. The story I liked best was the one that had her in a lunatic asylum stabbing scissors into footballs, drooling and screaming, 'Are you Jaryd Kiffing?' at all the visitors. That was my favourite, but as I made it up myself, you could say I was biased.

Naturally, Kiffo took all the credit for getting rid of her. For a while he was the envy of the school. Even Year 12 students looked on him with respect. As if he'd attacked a heavily fortified enemy encampment with only a rusty tin-opener and wiped out an entire battalion. He was a legend. He told me later that his dad tried to sue the Education Department for a million dollars. When he found out that this was going to be a little difficult, his dad offered to forget the whole matter for a slab of beer and two hundred smokes. A bit difficult after that climb down to remain a credible plaintiff.

Yeah, he had a good few weeks did Kiffo. But then Miss Payne appeared. And Jaryd Kiffing was a marked man. You see, Miss Payne was a different type of teacher entirely. If Miss Leanyer was the Snow White of the educational world, Miss Payne was the slash 'em up homicidal maniac. And Kiffo was home alone, and the phone lines had been cut.

DECEMBER: Primary school, Year 6.

The sky is swollen, the air heavy with darkness and the promise of rain. You skip down the stairs to the toilet block. In your right hand is a note signed by your teacher. You are all thin legs and arms and gingham school uniform. You pause outside the boys' toilets, head cocked to one side, listening. From within, there is a dull thudding, as regular as a metronome. You stand for a while, hesitant.

'Is anyone there?' you ask, but there is no reply. The thudding continues. You enter the darkness of the toilets. Your heart is hammering in your flat chest because you know that you shouldn't be there. Not in the boys' toilets. Not with that thudding threat. There is a thick smell of stale urine. It makes your eyes water but you move further in. There is a urinal on your right. Empty. Further along there is a row of cubicles. The thudding is coming from the one furthest away. The door is open. You move slowly towards it.

'Who's there?' you ask.

Silence, apart from the thudding. It forms a counterpoint with the beating of your heart. You want to run, but you also need to see. It seems to take an age, but you reach the corner of the door. You peer slowly round it, matchstick legs tensed for flight.

Chapter 2

So just how many friends has John Marsden got?

'Creeping hell!' said Vanessa. 'What in the name of God is that?'

I was bent over my exercise book, putting the final touches to a character star sign entry, when her hoarse whisper caught my attention. I looked up at her face. Her eyes were glazed with horror and her mouth turned down in an expression that seemed to indicate that something exceptionally smelly had just been thrust under her nose. Naturally, I twisted my head to follow her line of sight. And when I saw what she had seen, my jaw hit the desk . . .

Whoa! Hang on a moment. Let's take a break here. To be honest, I'm a complete beginner when it comes to story-telling and I need to take a time-out. Collect my thoughts. Sorry.

Tell me something. Have you ever read John Marsden's *Everything I Know About Writing*? Rhetorical question! Of course, I could sit here until you answer, though I suspect that

might take a long time. Sudden image of me sitting in the library for years waiting for the reply. I'm a skeleton in the corner, crumbling into dust, with a little sign on my ribcage saying, 'Still waiting for a reply'.

New students come to the school: 'What's with the skeleton?'

Librarian: 'She was writing a book. Asked a rhetorical question. Still waiting for a reply.'

Anyway, the reason I mention old John's book is that there was a bit in there that went something along the lines of, 'Just tell the story as if you were telling it to a friend.' I'm not sure if they were the exact words, but frankly I can't be bothered to look it up. You can, if you're interested. I thought at the time that this was good advice. It sounds easy enough. Now I've started, though, it seems trickier than I thought. I mean, I don't know you at all. I wouldn't recognise you from a hole in the ground. If I was telling this story to some friends, then they would already know Jaryd Kiffing and they would know me and they would know the school and everything. I'd just be able to get straight into what happened with Miss Payne. But you don't know anything. No offence. And that means I'll have to tell you about things that I wouldn't have to tell a friend.

Maybe John Marsden is friends with everyone in the world. But I don't think so. I've never had a phone call from him, for example. Unless it was that wrong number a couple of weeks ago.

I suppose I should tell you something about Jaryd Kiffing.

Kiffo. He is the most important player in this story, the chief character, the main *protagonist*. It's a great word, *protagonist*. I love it. There are some words, I've decided, that have to be written in italics. Or in bold, underlined. **Protagonist** is one.

Anyway, Kiffo. I could say all that stuff about how he is fifteen years old, of medium height, of limited academic ability and concentration span, with behavioural problems and freckles. The trouble is, that doesn't give you a clue what he is really like. The thing is, Kiffo isn't a character in a book. He's a real person. A friend, God help me. When I think about describing him, I just know that 'average height' and 'freckles' won't do it.

You remember that assignment on similes? My teacher hated what I wrote, but I was pretty pleased with it. She thought I was being too smart. How can you be too smart, by the way? Most of the time your teachers are telling you that you're being really dumb. 'Stop acting so stupid!' they say. And then when you do something intelligent, they say, 'Are you trying to be smart? Don't get smart with me, young lady.' I wish they'd make up their minds.

I got an afternoon detention for that simile assignment. Now I don't mind detentions. But I also got the whole, 'You are wasting a great talent. You should apply yourself, young lady,' lecture, which was really boring. I'm good at English, you see. Everyone thinks so. That's one reason me and Kiffo agreed that

I should write down the whole business about him and Miss Payne. But my teacher wanted me to be good in *her* way. Do you know what I mean? Take the simile assignment. I liked it. I really did. I thought it was funny, but also accurate. I'd put effort into it. But she wanted something else entirely. She had often told us to be original, but when I did something that was original, she went red in the face and steam hissed from her ears. Did she want me to be original in the same way as everyone else? Doesn't make much sense to me.

Anyway, I'm starting to wander away from the point. Jaryd Kiffing, fifteen, uglier than a bucketful of butt-holes, flaming red hair, bandy legs, really bad in all lessons, a waster, a hoon, disruptive, childish, violent at times, often cruel, class idiot, proud of his cultivated image of stupidity, part-time criminal. My friend.

And me? Well, I hope you might be a little curious about me, since I'm the one talking to you. My name is Calma Harrison and you can forget all the jokes about my first name. I've heard every single one. 'You need to be calmer, Calma,' or, 'You'll suffer from bad karma, Calma,' and all of that. The biggest thing about me is my boobs. I'm fifteen years old and my boobs are really huge. It's not that I'm overweight or anything. It's just that I seem to be saddled with a chest you could balance a tray on. As you can imagine, I'm a little self-conscious about this. Particularly in a Year 10 class filled with lads who are not exactly backward about making personal comments. I always wear baggy tops (uncomfortable, to say the least, in the heat of the tropics) but it still looks like I've got a couple of wombats tucked down there. If I turn quickly I'm liable to knock someone unconscious. You can probably imagine the kind of comments I've been getting. Not very original, of course. Things like, 'How many of those do you get to the kilo?' and, 'Can I park my bike in there?' and that sort of stuff. I hate PE, of course. I wasn't built for sudden movements. When I run, my chest stops half an hour after everything else.

Anyway, enough about my boobs. I just thought I should be honest about myself and that's the thing about me that I'm most aware of. And everyone else, apparently. As for the rest of me, well, I'm reasonably normal to look at. Fairly attractive, I suppose. Long dark hair that comes halfway down my back. None on my head, just down my back. Joke! Shortsighted, so I wear glasses. I like glasses. I've got about five pairs. The ones I like best at the moment (I keep changing my mind) are bright blue, thick plastic things. They are so in-your-face. And on your face, I guess. They do stand out like a nun in a betting shop. Maybe I reckon that if everyone is staring at my glasses, then they won't be looking at my chest. Isn't psychology great?

I'm a fairly hard worker at the subjects I enjoy, like English. Other stuff doesn't really interest me too much. Science is OK because it's quite beautiful and well worked out, like a poem.

And some of the words are really cool. But PE sucks. I hate physical exercise and I can't see the point of it. And while we're on the subject of pointlessness, can anyone explain the value of Drama lessons? Swaying like a tree or holding sweaty hands in a circle or pretending you're a bird. Call that adequate development of lifelong learning skills?

Q. And what makes you think you will be a good journalist/ teacher/copywriter/politician/organised crime boss?

A. *Well, even though I'm crap at reading and writing, I can do one hell of an impersonation of a sulphur-crested cockatoo in a cyclone.*

Look, I don't want to give the impression that I'm a rebel or anything. I tend to do what the teachers tell me to do because it's easier that way. I'm not like Kiffo in that sense. He seems to think that anything the teachers want you to do is a direct challenge to do the opposite. That's OK, though. We're all different. I just keep my head down and my chest in.

That's probably enough for the time being. I'll get back to the story.

Oh, hang on. There is one other thing you just might find interesting. Then again, maybe you won't. Who can tell? Anyway, here is another interesting/boring revelation about Calma Harrison: my mother is a Hotpoint refrigerator.

So where was I?

Chapter 3
Enter the Pit Bull

'Creeping hell!' said Vanessa. 'What in the name of God is that?'

I was bent over my exercise book, putting the final touches to a character star sign entry –

[**Vanessa Aldrick – Scorpio.** You seem to labour under the delusion that wearing appalling 1960s clothing and affecting an air of considerable boredom makes you an interesting and mysterious character whereas you are, in fact, a royal pain in the arse.]

– when her hoarse whisper caught my attention. I looked up at her face. Her eyes were glazed with horror and her mouth turned down in an expression that seemed to indicate that something exceptionally smelly had just been thrust under her nose. Vanessa would have yawned if the Archangel Gabriel had materialised in front of her on a skateboard, so naturally I twisted my head to follow her line of sight. When I saw what she had seen my jaw hit the desk . . .

Imagine a pit bull chewing a wasp and you'll have some idea of Miss Payne's expression when she entered our classroom the day after Miss Leanyer's dramatic departure. And I'm not talking about a normal, plug-ugly pit bull. I mean a pit bull that wasn't only at the end of the queue when looks were being dished out, but a pit bull that had missed the line altogether. The whole class gasped. One or two of the boys, the ones who spent all their time in the library playing chess, were on the point of passing out entirely. I'm fairly certain Melanie Simpson wet her knickers. I couldn't blame her. The vision in front of us would have made Attila the Hun soil his pants.

Miss Payne paced backwards and forwards at the front of the class for a few minutes. Built like a Russian shot-put champion, even her bulging biceps had muscles on them. The walls of the classroom shook as she paced, and small wisps of plaster drifted from the ceiling. She was wearing an enormous black dress that could have doubled as a six-person tent. We are talking an imposing presence! But it was her face that held our attention most. Small, red, beady eyes darted here and there, looking for the slightest sign of disruption. Fat chance.

24

None of us would have blinked if we'd been plugged into the mains electricity. A thick forest of eyebrow hair matched a bushy growth on her upper lip. Her mouth was twisted into a sneer, with little beads of drool starting to dribble. I mean, if she really had been a dog someone would have shot her before she had the chance to bite anyone.

After a minute or two, she stopped pacing and stood, like a brick wall, in the centre of the classroom, completely blotting out the blackboard. I could hear the ticking of the clock on the wall. Finally, the thin lips parted and she spoke. Imagine a voice that has the quality of rough sandpaper rubbing over solid granite and you will get the general idea.

'My name is Miss Payne,' she growled. 'You will address me either as "Miss" or "Miss Payne" or "Generalissimo" or "Führer". [I made those last two up.] Anyone who speaks without being asked will receive a detention. Any moving around without permission will incur a detention. Any slacking of any kind,' and here she swept her formidable gaze across the entire class, 'will incur a detention. No extensions of any kind will be granted for assignments. Late submission will result in a mark of zero and a detention. Any unauthorised consumption of any material whatsoever will result in a detention. Any lateness, for any reason whatsoever, will result in a detention. Unauthorised breathing, smiling and generally enjoying yourself will result in ritual disembowelment and a detention. [I made that up, as well.] Do I make myself clear?'

The silence within the class was broken by a strangled sob from somewhere at the back and the faint drip, drip, drip from Melanie Simpson's knickers. Miss Payne stepped forward, rattling the desks, and drew herself up to her full height of something in excess of two metres.

'I said, do I make myself clear?'

Thirty kids reacted as one.

'Yes, Miss.'

'Yes, Miss what?'

'Yes, Miss Payne.'

'That's better. Now get your books out. Failure to get your books out at the beginning of each lesson will result in a detention. Do not forget to bring writing materials. Failure to do so will result in a detention.'

Call me silly, if you like, but I was beginning to think that the notion of detention was becoming a recurrent linguistic motif.

'Now, I have been given some information about this class.' Miss Payne resumed her pacing. 'It has been brought to my attention that this is a particularly poor class in terms of attitude and work rate. This will change immediately. I have also heard that you have a history of treating teachers badly. In particular, your last teacher received totally unacceptable treatment at your hands. I will not tolerate any repetition, or attempted repetition, of such behaviour. Should you attempt to do so,' and there could be no doubt that her eyes were riveted to Jaryd Kiffing at this point, 'then you will regret it. I promise you that. Do your work and behave yourselves and you will find me, if not friendly and *fuzzy*, then at least tolerable. Cross me and you'll wish you had never been born. Right, spelling test. Thirty commonly misspelled words. Anyone getting fewer than twenty words correct will receive a detention. First word – "iridescent".'

I got twenty-nine. 'Diarrhoea' was the only stain on an otherwise clean sheet. Kiffo got one. Pretty remarkable. I would have put money on him getting a big fat zero. Actually, over half the class got fewer than twenty. I mean, they were *tough* words. At least two thirds were words that the likes of Kiffo had never even heard, let alone read. It was a little unfair. Still, never mind. I was OK.

Of course, I was interested to see what Miss Payne would do with over half the class. You couldn't give that many kids a detention.

I was wrong.

'I will see you eighteen here at lunchtime,' she said, 'and we'll go over those words again. Now, quiet reading for the rest of the lesson.'

I've already told you that I love English, but I was really glad when the bell finally went for recess. I'd often thought that a quiet classroom would be great – concentrate on the work, do some uninterrupted reading without Kiffo recreating one of the battles of Gallipoli with the other boys at the back of the class. But it was strange. The silence was complete, but it wasn't a silence that felt right, somehow. It was strained to the point that you couldn't even read without the pressure forcing itself into your consciousness. I suppose that at least I'd learned there can be different types of silence. When the bell did go, we all looked up at Miss Payne and waited for her to dismiss us. Normally there would have been a rush for the door and the smaller members of the class would be in physical danger of getting trampled to death. Not today. Miss Payne glowered at us for about thirty seconds.

'I'm waiting for complete quiet,' she said.

Complete quiet? You'd have got more noise in an insulated coffin. Maybe someone was doing some unauthorised breathing. Finally, we were allowed to file out, dazed and blinking. Without any conscious decision we formed a large group on the oval. The sun was beating fiercely through the trees, sending shivers of reflected light from the discarded Coke cans and foil wrappers that artistically dotted the grass. It was time for a committee meeting, though for a while we stood there in stunned silence.

'What a bitch!' said Melanie Simpson finally.

'A bitch?' chipped in Natalie Sykes. 'That's unfair on bitches, that is! If I was a bitch, I'd sue you for that comment.'

'You *are* a bitch, Natalie,' said Nathan Manning.

'Stuff you, Nathan,' replied Natalie.

'In your dreams, bitch.'

[**Natalie Sykes – Libra.** You are a poisoned dwarf with a face like a kicked-in peach.]

[**Nathan Manning – Sagittarius.** If acne were brains, you would be an intellectual heavyweight.]
[As a couple, romantically speaking, you are ideally suited, if only on the grounds that it is much better to make two people miserable than four.]

'Hang on, hang on.' I felt that it was important to get back to the agenda. 'We're not here to have a go at each other. What about the Pit Bull back there?'

There was a chorus of agreement.

'Yeah, right. What a bitch!'

'She's a bitch, all right.'

'A real bitch, that one.'

I felt we weren't making much progress.

'OK.' I said. 'No need for a secret ballot on that motion. The *real* point, though, is what are we going to do about her?'

There was much rueful shaking of heads and scratching behind ears. We'd had no problem establishing that Miss Payne was of the canine persuasion, but survival tactics were a different matter. Kiffo, who rarely attended class meetings since he normally lost no time at recess in kicking a footy around and building up a store of body odour for the rest of the morning, was prominent in the rueful scratching stakes. The silence deepened.

'I think,' said Nathan finally, the fruits of his deliberations breaking through to the cratered surface of his face, 'I think she's a real bitch.'

'A valid point, Nathan,' I said, 'and one that you make with your customary level of articulation. But, I repeat: what are we going to do?'

'I wonder what her first name is,' said Natalie. 'Ima. Ima Payne. That's it!'

There was general chuckling and fifteen minds bent themselves towards this amusing notion.

'I.B.A. Payne,' said Melanie Simpson.

'Wotta Payne,' said Kiffo, rather unconvincingly.

'Doris Payne,' said Nathan.

There was a silence.

'What do you mean "Doris Payne"?' said Julie Walker. 'That doesn't make sense!'

'I had an Aunt Doris once,' said Nathan. 'And she was a real bitch as well.'

I tell you, at my school, it's hard to keep up with the white heat of intellectual debate.

'Anyway,' Kiffo chipped in, with no regard to the conversational etiquette of keeping to the subject in hand, 'I'm not going to go to no detention. No way. I've never been to no detention no time and there's no way I'm going to no detention now.'

Running out of double negatives, he lapsed into brooding silence. Fortunately, the bell rang for class. I felt that progress had been minimal and the way things were going, it was unlikely to be more fruitful if recess had been extended. At least Kiffo was going to make a stand, though. I felt grateful for that. Vanessa and I made our thoughtful way towards the Science block.

'What do you reckon, Vanessa?' I asked.

Vanessa slowly turned her face towards me.

'About what?'

'About Miss Payne!'

'Who?'

'The Hound of the Baskervilles, the English teacher from Hell. The Pit Bull!'

'I wasn't really listening,' she drawled and floated off in the direction of Maths, trailing a little dark cloud of boredom behind her.

Kiffo looked lost at lunchtime. True to his word, he hadn't turned up to Miss Payne's detention. He walked around the oval, kicking his footy in splendid isolation. He was a forlorn figure. I was looking forward to the next English class. It seemed to me that battle lines had been well and truly drawn and the contest could be pretty equal. Of course, at that time I had no idea how it would all turn out. I remember thinking that even though Miss Payne could probably disembowel a horse with her teeth, the odds were still with Kiffo. I don't mean in a straight physical fight. I doubt if anyone without a black belt in five of the martial arts would stand much of a chance against the Pit Bull. But physical strength counts for nothing when it's a teacher against a student. Base animal cunning, emotional ruthlessness and a complete lack of any moral fibre will always win out. Put that way, I couldn't see how Kiffo could fail. It was going to get interesting, though. There was no doubt in my mind about that. Unfortunately, I had to wait until the following day for the next English lesson. Fortunately, it was first up after Home Group.

The door crashed open and the Pit Bull swept into the room. Once again we were treated to five minutes of red-eyed glowering and the menacing body posture of a sumo wrestler. She oozed down the aisles, darting glances from side to side, impaling with a steely gaze anyone who looked as if they might be beginning to get the first hazy notion of wrong-doing. Finally, she came to a halt in front of Kiffo's desk. Spreading her feet, she leaned forward and placed both fists onto the desk. It groaned in protest. Then there was silence.

'Jaryd Kiffing,' she said ominously, her voice low and charged with violence. 'You didn't make detention yesterday. I am interested in your excuse. Not that it will be acceptable, of course. You must understand that. But tell me, Mr Kiffing. Was your absence due to amnesia or should I read something more sinister into it?'

Kiffo mumbled something.

'I'm sorry, Mr Kiffing. I didn't quite catch that.'

'The test was too hard.'

'The test was too hard. Was it? Was it indeed? And what makes you say that, Mr Kiffing? Is that conclusion the result of years of scholarly research, the product of a degree in teaching or just the complaint of a lazy, revolting adolescent? What's your considered opinion, Mr Kiffing?'

'You're being unfair, Miss Payne!'

God, where did that voice come from? I looked around the class before I realised that it was me. What had I done?

Miss Payne swivelled around and fixed me with her eyes. For a moment, nothing happened. Then, slowly and deliberately, she moved between the desks and stood before me.

'You have an opinion, Miss Harrison? Pray, share it with us.'

I swallowed hard. The easiest thing to do, I knew it even then, would have been to bow my head and mumble, 'Nothing, Miss.' But I couldn't. Always been my problem, I guess. A mouth that sometimes works independently of my brain. My voice sounded unnaturally calm.

'I think you are overestimating Jaryd Kiffing's linguistic capacity, Miss. You fail to appreciate the effect of a dysfunctional family unit operating within his socio-economic background upon an intellect that has never been given the opportunity to flourish. Those thirty words, Miss. Kiffo wouldn't have heard twenty-eight of them in his entire life. The Kiffing household does not treasure academic success, nor does it encourage excellence in anything other than excessive drinking and flatulence. Kiffo has, to my certain knowledge, never read a book in his life. I doubt, even now, if he could colour one in satisfactorily. Your test, Miss, was a guarantee of failure for Kiffo and those like him. It might as well have been in Swahili or Serbo-Croatian. It was, by any academic and intellectual standard, grossly unfair.'

Phew! Where did that come from? Calma, girl, you are a never-ending source of amazement and wonder, especially to me. I sat back, pretty proud of myself but also conscious that I had probably just dropped myself deep in the brown and smelly stuff. Miss Payne's eyes twitched. For a moment, I thought she was going to throttle me. A little vein stood out on her temple. I could see the blood pumping through it. With a massive sigh, as though the effort of controlling herself was almost more than she could bear, Miss Payne straightened up. Her piggy eyes moved in a broad sweep and took in my glasses (I was wearing the bright green plastic ones) then travelled down my whole form. I felt like a fly that was about to be swatted.

'Well, Miss Harrison, that was quite a speech. Yes, indeed. I'm not sure if I have ever heard the like in my entire teaching career. However . . .' She suddenly yelled into my face with such force that it felt like a physical blow. It was like being caught up in a mini cyclone. Even Vanessa woke up. 'HOW-

EVER, you would be well advised to keep your smart remarks to yourself in future. When I want your opinion, then I will ask for it. Is that understood?'

'But you did ask for it! You said, "Pray share it with us."'

'SHUT UP!!'

Miss Payne thumped about the room like a raging, maddened bull.

'This is exactly the kind of behaviour I was talking about yesterday! I will not have you answering me back. I will not be disobeyed. Kiffing and Harrison. You will come here tomorrow for an after-school detention. You, Kiffing, for not turning up yesterday, and you, Harrison, for insubordination. Now get out your English grammar books and turn to page thirty-three. You will answer the section on apostrophes. You will work, of course, in complete silence.'

Kiffo caught up with me at recess. I was a bit concerned at first. I thought he probably wanted to beat me up because of the comments I'd made about his home life. You can't tell with him sometimes. As it turned out, I didn't have to worry. He'd come to thank me. Mind you, it wasn't something he was particularly comfortable with.

'Wassup, Kiffo?' I said.

'Wassup, four-eyes?' he replied.

'You and me for detention, huh?'

'Not me! I'm not going. She can get stuffed. I'm not staying behind after normal hours. No chance. No way my dad will give permission. I can tell you that for nothing. Bitch. No, I just wanted to say thanks . . . you know, for sticking up for me.'

'Think nothing of it, Kiffo.'

'No. I do. Think something of it, I mean. You didn't have to do it. And I just wanted you to know . . . well, I just wanted you to know that you're a good mate.'

'Hey, Kiffo,' I said. 'We'll always be good mates. How could we be anything else?'

'Oh, by the way,' he said. 'I did colour in a book. Last week. And it was pretty good. Mostly.'

I looked at him, but his expression was blank. That's the thing with Kiffo. Sometimes you don't have a clue whether he's being serious, or sending you up. Then I caught a faint sparkle in his eyes and it occurred to me, not for the first time, that if Kiffo didn't exist, I'd have to invent him.

I grinned.

And that was it, really. I didn't give the whole business with Kiffo and the Pit Bull much more thought. I turned up to the detention the following day, prepared to do my time. I certainly wasn't expecting Kiffo to be there. But he was. And he was ropeable.

DECEMBER: Primary school, Year 6.

There is a red-haired boy sitting on the floor beside the toilet bowl, his left arm draped over the stained porcelain. Tears pour down the freckled map of his face but his expression is blank. His right arm is swinging rhythmically across his knees, his fist smashing into the cubicle wall, sinking into the hole that has resulted from the regular punching. The boy's hand is covered in blood, and you can see that it is broken and swollen.

You're frightened, not so much by the violence, but by the calm manner in which it is being inflicted. You crouch down and touch the boy gently on the knee.

'Are you OK?' You instantly feel ashamed at the stupidity of the question. The boy looks up but doesn't change his routine. The fist slams into the wall again. He doesn't flinch.

'Fuck off,' he says, without malice.

You run. You run to find a teacher. You run to tell your story of a boy, a toilet and a fist that will hammer inside your head forever.

Chapter 4
Conversations with the refrigerator

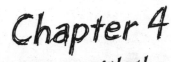

Dear Fridge,

The casserole was great! Thanks. However, I feel that our intimate dinner was something of a flop. I made the effort, God knows. Candles, mood music. But, frankly, you were not receptive to my conversational overtures. In fact, solid presence though you undoubtedly are in my life, I sometimes feel that our relationship is not what it once was.

We need to talk.

In the meantime, my new English teacher, a charming woman of considerable charisma, has requested my presence at an after-school meeting tomorrow. Would you be so kind as to sign the attached permission slip?

Your loving daughter,

Calma

Dear Calma,

Permission slip signed. What have you been up to?
Can you heat up a pizza for dinner tonight? I'm on
late shift at the supermarket, so I'll have to go
straight to the pub. Will be home about two. Don't
wake me, please.
Can you cut out the sarcasm in the notes? To be
honest, I'm too tired to deal with it.

Love,

Mum

Dear Fridge,

How can you be so cold-hearted?
Love,

Calma

Chapter 5
Crime and punishment,
part one

Two bloody hours! That's how long the detention was! I couldn't believe it. It wasn't even as if there was any educational value. Kiffo and I weren't told to do any work. In fact, we were expressly forbidden from reading. Not that Kiffo would have wanted to read, but I certainly did. We just had to sit there, at opposite ends of the classroom, staring at the front where the Pit Bull was marking exercise books. Have you any idea how long two hours is? Yeah, well, I know it's like one hundred and twenty minutes and all that. Don't get smart with me. What I mean is, two hours feels much longer than one hundred and twenty minutes when all you have to do is stare at the wall. And believe me, when the alternative to the wall is staring at Miss Payne, you'd choose the wall every time.

I did a lot of thinking. It was clear to me that the Pit Bull would have to go. There was no way the class could survive the rest of the year with her. We'd only had her less than a week and some kids were already on medication. Melanie Simpson had burst into tears twice while we were lined up outside the classroom. The whole situation was unacceptable. The problem was, how to get rid of her. Most times, the answer would be easy. I'll let you into a little secret here. Take an average Year 10 class, anywhere in the country, and I'll bet you ten dollars to a pinch of poo that they could get rid of their teacher if they wanted to badly enough. Yes, I know about teachers' working conditions and contracts and all that. But none of that makes any difference. Students can destroy the teacher's health, physical and emotional, if we want. We can induce nervous breakdowns. You see, we know that teachers have no rights. They can't hit us, they can't discipline us in any serious way, they can't even yell at us without the danger of a lawsuit. Whereas we, the students, can abuse the teacher, refuse to do what we are told to do, refuse to listen or refuse to stop talking. In fact, we can do whatever we like, short of physical violence (and that happens sometimes – sure, you can get expelled from school, but they still have to move you to another school. It's the law of the land. Even thugs below the school-leaving age are entitled to an education). Take thirty kids who are determined to destroy a teacher and there's not much anyone can do.

But the Pit Bull? I wasn't sure that any of the normal tactics would work with her. You need a weakness to work on and as far as I could tell, the Pit Bull had armour-plated skin and the sensitivity of a paving slab. I guess if we could have worked together then we might have stood a chance. After all, the same rules of conduct applied to her as they did to other teachers. The trouble was that most of the kids in the class were terrified of her. Well, we all were, to be honest with you. And that meant it was going to be difficult to present a united front when everyone was worried about his or her own personal safety. There had to be a way though. But at the end of two hours, I was no closer to finding it.

The Pit Bull gathered her papers together and glanced at the clock.

'You can go,' she said.

Kiffo and I stretched aching limbs and got painfully to our feet.

'Miss Harrison. I would like a word with you, if I may.'

Believe me, I felt that two hours was sufficient punishment, but what can you do? I sat down again as Kiffo opened the door and left. The Pit Bull finished shuffling her exercise books and then came and sat opposite me. Her expression was what is known as 'ruminative'.

'Calma,' she said, not unkindly. 'I've been reading the English work in your Year 10 folio. It is . . . well, how can one express it? Brilliant, I think, is not an over-exaggeration. I've been teaching for longer than I care to remember and very seldom, if ever, have I come across a talent like yours.' She fell silent and I squirmed.

'Thanks,' I said, rather inadequately. Let's be honest. It's difficult to be churlish when someone says you're brilliant.

'Do you think you have a gift for English?' she continued.

'Well, I try not to fly in the face of public opinion,' I replied, a little more adequately.

The Pit Bull frowned.

'No. There's no question about your talent,' she continued. 'It's your attitude that worries me.'

I squirmed again. It was one of those days when my squirmy muscles were going to get a good work-out. Attitude! What is it with teachers and attitude? My writing is good. Great! What has attitude got to do with the price of fish if the end product is good? I can just see some Elizabethan schoolteacher wagging his finger at Shakespeare. 'Sure, matey, I concede that *Hamlet* is the greatest piece of literature ever written. But it's your attitude that worries me!' I kept silent, though. When it comes to teachers and the subject of attitude, they're like a road train with brake failure on a long slope. There's nothing you can do until they stop rolling.

'And that attitude is not helped by the company you keep. Now, I don't want to tell you what friends you should have,' she said in exactly the manner of someone who is telling you what friends you should have, 'but I have had some dealings with Mr Kiffing's family and I know what I am talking about. It would be in your best interests to find ... more *suitable* companions. Friends who challenge you intellectually and who are not so – how can one put it? – antisocial in their personal lives.'

I bristled. What with the squirming and the bristling, it was quite an energetic end to my detention.

'Thank you, Miss. I'll keep that in mind.'

'I hope you do, Calma. I really hope you do.'

'Oh trust me. I won't forget. I can promise you that.'

I got to the door and was halfway through it before she spoke again.

'By the way, Calma,' she said. 'Loved the simile exercise.'

Huh! I felt like smacking her in the face. Might have improved it.

Kiffo was waiting for me when I came out.

'What did fart-face want, then?' he said.

'Oh nothing. Normal stuff, wasting talent, bad attitude, blah de blah.'

We walked together for a while, two jailbirds bonded by a common experience. I glanced occasionally at his face, which was even darker and more brooding than normal. I thought there was a danger in asking the question I had been dying to ask him, but I went ahead just the same.

'Kiffo?' I said. 'How come you turned up to that dumb detention? I thought your dad would never sign one of those permission slips.'

He stopped dead and turned towards me.

'Don't talk to me about that bastard! He signed it. Said Miss Payne had had a chat with him about my education and all that crap. Told me he wanted me to try harder at school-work! Yeah, right! First time he's ever shown any interest in anything you can't drink or smoke or punch.'

'So what would have happened if you hadn't turned up? I mean, it's not the first time you would've disobeyed your dad.'

Kiffo's hands pulled his tangled mop of red hair into crazier spikes. Boy, was he angry.

'He'd have beaten the crap out of me, all right? There's still a few years to go before he can't do that no more.'

'So what are we going to do, Kiffo? I mean, we can't carry on like this.'

'I know what I'm going to do,' he said quietly. 'I'm going to trash her house. I'm going to destroy everything that bitch owns.'

It was my turn to stop dead in my tracks. At this rate, we'd never make it home.

'Are you crazy, Kiffo? What good would it do? It wouldn't get rid of her. It would only make her more twisted and nasty. She'd probably figure out that it was a student – I don't think she's making too many friends here – and what do you reckon then? That she's going to be nicer to us? I don't think so. I think she'll be even worse.'

'I don't care. This isn't about getting rid of her. This is about revenge. This is personal, Calma.'

'You *are* out of your mind, Kiffo!' I said. 'What the hell are you talking about, "personal"?' It was hardly the first time a teacher had tried to put the screws on Kiffo. Most times he welcomed it. Gave him a challenge – you know, like a sporting event, two bruisers slugging it out for glory. But not personal. Never personal. Even the humiliation of a detention wasn't enough to make sense of what he was planning to do. Then I had a sudden thought, a connection.

'Kiffo?' I said.

He grunted.

'Does the Pit Bull know your family? I mean before she became our teacher? You know, in the past?'

There was just the slightest pause in Kiffo's step, but he kept walking, his head averted.

'You're kiddin',' he said finally. 'Just 'cos we mix with muggers and murderers doesn't mean we don't have standards.'

He looked at me and grinned. And I knew at that moment, knew it with a cold, hard certainty, that he was lying to me. I had no idea why and I didn't care. I was too busy tasting the cold lump of betrayal in my throat.

'Listen, kid,' he said brightly, 'I'd better get going.'

He squeezed me briefly on the arm and then he was gone. I watched him for a while, my hand on the spot where he had touched me. I considered heading off to Vanessa's house, but in the end I couldn't be bothered. I was too depressed. I did know one thing, however. Whatever Kiffo was up to, I was going to be a part of it as well. We were *friends*. And I wasn't going to let him lie to me and get away with it. No one, and I mean no one, treats Calma Harrison like that.

FEBRUARY: Primary school, Year 6.

You are sitting on a bench by the school oval. It is lunchtime. You open your lunch box and arrange the contents beside you on the bench. There is an apple, a bag of salt and vinegar crisps, a chicken sandwich and a chocolate biscuit. You suddenly notice a red-haired boy looking at the food. He is standing a little behind you. There is nothing in his hands. You pick up the bag of crisps and his eyes follow you.

'Are you hungry?' you ask.

He shrugs.

'Would you like these crisps?' you ask.

He shrugs.

He eats the crisps. Then he eats your sandwich and the biscuit. He turns down the apple. You don't mind. You're not very hungry anyway. When he has finished, he wanders on to the oval and joins in a game of footy. He has said nothing.

'You're welcome,' you say.

Chapter 6
Crime and punishment,
part two

The next week passed uneventfully. English classes were horrible, but we kept our heads down and put up with it. But even that didn't seem to satisfy the Pit Bull. She'd find the weakest reasons for singling out some of the kids. The way they looked at her. Noises they made that only she could hear. She set impossible tasks and then punished students for failing to complete them. It got so that you were grateful if she was picking on someone else. I hated that, the way she made us selfish, thankful that someone else was going through hell because it meant that you weren't suffering. That her attention was elsewhere. I got off pretty lightly, probably because I was 'gifted' and all that crap. And probably because I didn't stir her up.

Kiffo suffered the most. A lesson didn't go by without her tormenting him in one way or another. I really did feel sorry for him. OK, I know that Kiffo could be a real bastard. Maybe this was payback for all the times he had made teachers suffer, without ever thinking of their welfare. Who the hell knows? But there was no doubt that when the Pit Bull was working herself up into a frenzy, it was costing him. On many occasions he was really close to hitting her. I could tell. A glazed look would come into his eyes and his hands would tighten into fists. Sometimes, I thought that was exactly what the Pit Bull wanted. For him to have a go. But he didn't do anything. She told him that he was a loathsome sore on the backside of humanity, that he made pond slime appear intellectually advanced in comparison, that he was *nothing*, and he took it. Those kids who sat at the back of the class with Kiffo did nothing to help either. They kept their heads down and pretended they were invisible. That's what I mean. They were supposed to be his friends, but they were too busy looking out for themselves to give him any support. And all I did was stand by and watch the Pit Bull turn us into uncaring, I'm-all-right-Jack types. She was destroying our sense of what was right and what was wrong. She was turning us into politicians. The future of Australia deserved better than that.

Now, I know that Kiffo's plan for the Pit Bull wasn't exactly brilliant, that, in fact, it was wrong. That it wouldn't help in any way whatsoever. But I also knew that I was going to be a part of it. Listen, I'm just telling you the way things were, the way things had to be between me and Kiffo. I'm not asking for your approval.

I caught up with Kiffo on Friday at lunchtime. He was acting all nonchalant, which was exactly the wrong kind of approach with me. Honestly, men! They think they are so smart. And the more they try to be smart, the more they seem as dumb as a hammock full of hammers.

'So when are you doing this, Kiffo?' I said.

'Doing what?'

'You know what I mean,' I said.

'I don't know what you're talking about, Calma.'

I grabbed the front of his T-shirt and pulled his face towards mine.

'Listen, matey,' I said. 'There are two things you should never get confused about with me. First, I am not stupid. Second, I am not about to let a mate get himself in all sorts of strife without me there to help out. OK? Now, you can do this one of two ways. You can continue with your impersonation of a complete moron – and, incidentally, it's one you do with uncanny accuracy – and find me following you everywhere you go. Or you can just answer a straightforward question, which will save us both a lot of time. When are you going to trash the Pit Bull's place?'

Kiffo's face registered a look I recognised – the one that showed he knew he was going to be the loser if he argued with me. He gave it another go, mind you.

'Just drop it, Calma!'

'When?'

'I'm trying to protect you!'

'When?'

And then he sagged, like I knew he would.

'Tonight,' he said, eyes flicking about as if in search of support.

'So where do we meet?'

For a moment I thought he was going to start arguing again, but instead he gave a sigh. I knew I had won.

'All right, all right! Meet me at five-thirty outside Woolies in the mall. Have you got camouflage gear?'

'Bloody hell, Kiffo,' I said. 'This isn't World War Three!'

'It is to me. Never mind. Be on time, right?'

Throughout the entire afternoon, I was in a nervous frenzy. I'll admit it. I actually thought it was really exciting. But I knew there was a line I wouldn't cross. There was no way I was going into the Pit Bull's house. I'd watch out for Kiffo, but any breaking and entering would be up to him. I told him that much when we met at five-thirty.

'God, Calma,' he said. 'As if I'd let you break in! You'd probably get your tits stuck in the window. No. Listen, just watch out for me, right? Keep guard.'

He looked me up and down.

'Is that the best you could do?'

Under the circumstances, I thought I had done pretty well. Dark blue jeans and a maroon singlet. Kiffo looked like something out of a survival video for bush weirdos. He had head-to-toe camouflage gear, heavy black boots and a black balaclava perched like a beanie on the top of his head. I mean, really anonymous when you're hanging around outside K-Mart on a Friday afternoon! All the mothers with kids in buggies were going past looking at Kiffo like he was Osama bin Laden.

'I thought the idea with camouflage gear was to blend in with the surroundings,' I said to him, 'not stand out like a marine in a nunnery. You would have been better off hiring a buggy and a couple of kids.'

Kiffo looked a little indignant.

'Yeah, well. It stands out here, doesn't it? But it won't stand out in the Pit Bull's yard, will it? Come on, we'd better get going.'

We left the mall and walked off towards the southern suburbs. It was already starting to get dark which, to be perfectly honest, suited me down to the ground. Now that we had started on this, I was nervous and didn't like the idea of anyone spotting me with Kiffo, particularly dressed the way he was. I had visions of an episode of *Crimestoppers*.

Close-up of smooth, good-looking bastard with anal-retentive hair and discreet tie. He could be one of those models you see in catalogues, flanked by a couple of clean-cut clones sporting seriously

unpleasant leisure garments. There is a Crimestoppers logo perched over his immaculate left shoulder: 'Can anyone remember seeing two young people near the mall between five-thirty and six on the evening of the seventeenth of May? A young male, aged about fifteen with camouflage gear, bandy legs, bright red hair with a beanie stuck on the top like a black cherry. His accomplice had huge boobs and orange glasses the size of up-and-over garage doors.'

No, the gathering dark was just fine with me.

Kiffo was moving like a man possessed. I had a struggle to keep up with him.

'How did you find out where she lived, Kiffo?' I panted.

'Easy,' he replied. 'Borrowed my mate's motorbike. Followed her home from school.'

'What are we going to do when we get there? I mean, for all we know, she could spend her evenings doing crosswords or pulling the wings off butterflies or sharpening her teeth. I can't imagine she has a loving circle of friends. And what if she has family?' I really couldn't imagine the Pit Bull having family, mind you. She wasn't born, she was quarried. Nonetheless, I thought it was unlikely that she'd be out of an evening dancing at the local club or taking embroidery classes. I could see us sitting outside her house most of the night with nothing to show for it.

'It's sorted,' said Kiffo. 'She's got a dog.'

'A dog?' I repeated. This was getting worse. 'How does that help us?'

'She takes it for a walk. Every night, the same time. Seven to eight-thirty. You can set your watch by it. Plenty of time for me to be in there, out again and both of us to be home before she gets halfway through exercising the mutt. Trust me.'

I shivered, even though the evening was uncomfortably warm. This was Kiffo's thing, his expertise. In the classroom, I was the boss. I knew my way around a poem. He knew his way around other people's houses. I thought about the different worlds we inhabited and wondered how I had managed to get myself involved in his.

We eventually stopped outside a small, low-set house in a nondescript area of the city. Kiffo and I stood across the road under a large casuarina where we were reasonably safe from prying neighbours. He hunkered down and pulled a pack of cigarettes from his camouflage jacket. He offered me one. I shook my head. I was developing enough bad habits for one evening. Aiding and abetting a break-in, an accomplice to a serious crime, a gangster's moll. Kiffo lit up and looked across the road with narrowed eyes. I wasn't sure if this was because of the smoke or because he thought it was tough. I crouched down beside him and practised narrowing my eyes. He pointed at the house with his cigarette.

'Ten minutes. Then she'll be gone. All you gotta do is watch out for anyone who might be suspicious and let me know. I'll only be in there ten minutes. Piece of cake.'

'Yeah,' I said, 'and just how am I supposed to let you know if someone does get suspicious? Set off fireworks, use a loud-hailer, assemble a marching band?'

Kiffo narrowed his eyes further. God, I wished I could do that. I made a resolution to practise. He kept silent for a while, and with one of those horrible sinking feelings, I realised that this was something he hadn't given much thought to. I guess I shouldn't have been surprised.

'You'll think of something,' he replied finally, showing more faith in me than I could summon. 'Anyway, quiet. Here she is.'

I wasn't encouraged by the fact that she was eight minutes early according to Kiffo's calculations. Maybe he wasn't too fussy when it came to setting his watch. Maybe he couldn't tell the time. Not that it mattered. I watched as the Pit Bull opened the front door of her house and came out, trying to restrain the biggest dog I had ever seen in my life. I mean this thing was *huge*. And it looked as bad-tempered as hell. So would I if I had to share living space with the Pit Bull, mind. Even so, this was clearly a dog with limited things on its mind. Like ripping people to shreds, for example. It strained at the lead as if anxious to find someone in need of shredding, its bulging muscles gleaming in the porch light. By now, the evening had settled and the dark was profound. There was nothing behind us except a sports oval and I knew that from the Pit Bull's point of view we would have been lost in the gloom beneath the tree. I was worried about the dog, though. Maybe it would smell us. Hell, the way I was sweating, Miss Payne could have smelled me. I nudged slightly closer to Kiffo as the Pit Bull struggled with the gate. The dog was so keen to get out for a walk that it nearly pulled her arm through the chain links. I smiled as Miss Payne swore, but the smile froze on my lips when she smacked the dog around the head with one huge fist. The poor old pooch damn near collapsed. You could see the stars circling around its head. Now this dog looked like it could savage and eat an entire army battalion and still have room for dessert, but it was clear who was the boss in the household. The dog whined and cowered as the Pit Bull raised her voice.

'Down, Slasher, down. Blast you.'

Slasher! Talk about the pot calling the kettle black. I felt hugely sorry for the hound then. Even though it was built like a JCB, it stood no chance against the Pit Bull. I knew how it felt. Kiffo and I crouched together and watched as the two brutes thundered down the road. The last I saw of the dog was when it bulldozed around a corner, under a streetlight, almost leaving gouges in the pavement. Kiffo had been cupping his cigarette in his hand, shielding the glow. Now he took a final drag and threw the butt on to the road. He stood up and pulled the balaclava over his head. Normally I would have considered this a blessing. Kiffo's face was not exactly a thing of beauty and a joy forever. But now there was something extremely menacing about him. I felt scared. Of him, of the dark, of what we were about to do. I wanted to turn and run, but it was too late. Kiffo pulled me closer to him and whispered urgently.

'Keep an eye out. I'll be ten minutes, tops.'

And he was gone. He slipped into the dark, across the road, and was through the Pit Bull's gate before I could say anything. I caught a quick glimpse of his small figure as it moved around the side of the house. I realised that I had been holding my breath and I let it go in a long, slow exhalation.

To be honest I was panicking. It might sound like an easy job, just standing under a tree looking around, but I felt the eyes of the world upon me. What would I do if a police car pulled up? What excuse would I have for standing under a casuarina tree in a quiet residential area? I know it's not a crime, but it's a strange thing to do, isn't it? I tried to get further into the shadow, but I was also conscious that I needed a clear view of the road both ways. I was starting to wish I had put on a different pair of glasses. Were these ones luminous? I couldn't remember but they certainly felt like they were glowing. I could imagine curious neighbours ringing the police and saying, 'Please come at once. The casuarina tree across the road is wearing glasses and it's starting to spook me.'

I needed to empty my bladder as well. Could I risk it here? Knowing my luck, I'd be caught with my knickers around my ankles and that *would* be a hard one to explain away. I swivelled my eyes from one side of the street to the other. The least movement made my head snap around. I was starting to get dizzy and I felt sick. How long was he going to be in there? I glanced at my watch and saw that he had been gone for exactly a minute! The whole concept of time was messing my head up.

And then I froze. I couldn't believe it. Around the corner, like a shaggy tank, appeared Slasher, followed in quick succession by the vast bulk of the Pit Bull. My tongue spot-welded itself to the roof of my mouth and my legs turned to cottage cheese.

What the hell was I going to do now? For one wild moment, I thought that maybe she had gone the wrong way and was simply re-tracing her steps to pass the house and go in the opposite direction. Yeah, right! The streetlights etched her face in sharp relief and I shuddered. She was coming back. God knows why, but it looked like walkies was finished for today. What was it Kiffo had said? An hour and a half. You could set your watch by it. What an idiot!

The Pit Bull was bearing down on me and I couldn't think of anything to do. I tried whispering 'Kiffo' really quietly until

I caught myself. We were in enough trouble with just one idiot around. Why hadn't we brought mobile phones? The fact that I didn't have one and neither did Kiffo was possibly one reason, but I was still faced with the problem of contacting him. And quickly. I had visions of the Pit Bull opening her front door and finding Kiffo peeing on her pet parrot or something. Think, Harrison. Think.

There was only one thing for it. As the Pit Bull approached the front gate, as she was reaching into her pocket and extracting her house keys, I rushed across the road.

'Miss Payne!' I yelled at the top of my voice. 'Fancy seeing you here!'

Slasher and the Pit Bull both turned to face me, and I have to admit that I quailed. One of them growled but I'm not sure which. I tried a bright happy smile, like I was meeting my best friend, but it felt as if my face was moulded from durable resin. Miss Payne's lip curled as she looked me up and down. Her expression was the same, I imagined, as if she had stood in something Slasher might have done on the pavement.

'Miss Harrison,' she said. 'This is an unexpected pleasure. Goodbye.'

She turned to go.

'Wait!' I yelled. 'Please don't go. I . . . I wanted to talk to you.'

The Pit Bull looked at me.

'Oh, yes,' she said. 'And what do you think we might have to talk about at this time on a Friday evening?'

I searched my brain.

'The homework. The English homework. I wanted to ask for your help. I remembered what you said about my attitude, Miss Payne, and I just wanted to show you that I was making an effort with it. My attitude, I mean. And the homework, of course.'

'I haven't set any homework, Miss Harrison.'

Crap!

'Exactly, Miss Payne. I wanted some homework and I knew you hadn't set any, not that I'm criticising or anything, I mean you must have your reasons for not setting homework, all that experience with teaching, I can tell you know exactly what you are doing, and so no homework is probably part of the big plan, something that is good for us, I mean, so I don't want you to think that by asking for homework I'm being insubordinate or anything 'cause that is certainly not my intention Miss Payne, good heavens, no.' I roared with laughter, shrieking at the top of my voice. Get the hell out of there, Kiffo! 'It's just that I love English, Miss Payne, and you make it so interesting that I felt it would be good, for me, I mean, to do some extra, it being Friday night and all and there being nothing I like better on a Friday than doing English homework, so I thought I'd ask you for some, homework, that is, and that's the help I referred to earlier.'

Miss Payne leaned forward so her face was within an inch of mine. Her breath smelled like a sumo wrestler's jockstrap.

'Miss Harrison, unless you go away now, I will call the police. Do I make myself plain?'

I was tempted to reply that something had indeed made her plain, and that I, personally, was inclined to blame her parents. Fortunately, I resisted the temptation.

'Well, to be honest, Miss,' I said, 'I'm not altogether clear on that point. When you say "the police" do you mean the regular . . . well, *police*, I suppose? Or do you mean something like the CID?'

I thought she was going to explode. A strangulated noise came from the back of her throat and her face filled with blood. In other circumstances, it would have been fascinating. I knew I couldn't keep this up for much longer or she'd kill me, so in a flash of inspiration I dropped to my knees in front of her bloody great slavering hound. The way to a pet owner's heart and all that.

'What a beautiful dog!' I said, peering into its bloodshot eyes. Its breath, I noticed, was almost as foul as its owner's. 'I just love dogs, don't you, Miss Payne, so sweet and . . .'

God knows how I would have carried on, but it was all academic since the dog, obviously mistaking me for some kind of huge doggy chew, made a lunge for my neck, its yellow fangs snapping shut with a sickening *clack* millimetres from my skin. I tumbled backwards and for a moment my life, such as it had been, flashed before my eyes. Take my word for it, it was no better the second time around. Slasher was straining at the leash, his eyes pinpricks of hatred. Only Miss Payne's grip on the leash kept the beast from ripping into me. I glanced up and I swear that she was thinking about letting it go. I looked into her eyes and I know she was giving it serious thought. If it did get loose, I was done for. One of us would have to die and there was no way I could kill that thing. Unless I got stuck in its throat, of course.

And then the moment passed. Miss Payne pulled back on the leash and raised her hand. Slasher instantly cowered. That made two of us. I leaped to my feet and tried the smile again. Even worse this time. Surely Kiffo would have had time to get out of there by now. I couldn't be sure.

'Anyway, Miss Payne, here I am prattling on about myself. That's enough about me. Let's talk about you. What do you think of me?'

'Miss Harrison, I don't know what game you are playing, but I have had enough.' Her voice was calm, but saturated in venom. 'You leap out in front of me and talk gibberish. If this is your idea of a joke, then I am afraid I don't get it. I have already had cause to talk to you about your attitude and now you accost me outside my home, presumably for some stupid practical joke that shows I was right to question your behaviour in the first place. I don't know how you found out where I live, but stalking is a crime and unless you leave now, you will be in more trouble than even your fertile mind could imagine. Now I am going into my home. My *home*, Miss Harrison. I don't expect to see you here again.'

And that was it, end of audience. She turned to go in through the gate and it was then, over her shoulder, that I saw the bedroom curtain twitch. That stupid bastard hadn't got out yet! Was he deaf as well as stupid? I had been making enough noise to wake my Uncle Jack and he had been dead these last ten years. Maybe I should have left him to it. I think I had done enough, I'm sure you'll agree. But it was another case of the mouth working while the brain was still having a lie-in.

'I love you, Miss Payne,' I yelled. 'I've fallen in love with you.'

That stopped her. Bloody well stopped me, too. Suddenly I was out of words. The Pit Bull turned and looked at me carefully. I tried to make a lovesick expression, but I think it just turned out sick.

'Are you serious?' she whispered.

'Never more so,' I found myself saying. 'I love everything about you, the way you move, the way your hair sort of . . .' I couldn't think what her hair might do other than fall down like a rusty sheet of corrugated iron. 'Everything,' I finished lamely. 'Perhaps we could talk about it. Perhaps we could go to a café and sit down and discuss it like adults.'

Miss Payne raised her hand and pointed a finger at me. It

was like a loaded gun.

'Go home, Miss Harrison,' she said. 'I will be reporting this incident to the Principal first thing on Monday morning. You need help and I will not speak to you further about this matter tonight.'

And that was it. She turned and, hauling the monstrous Slasher who looked as if he still had designs on the fleshier parts of my body, she disappeared into her house.

I waited around for ten or fifteen minutes, well away from the house, of course, to see if Kiffo had made it out in time. Nothing. Either he had snuck out the back and legged it for home or he was stuck in there with the Pit Bull. Whichever, there was nothing more I could do. I plodded home, feeling completely miserable. What had I done? Not only was I an accomplice in a serious crime – and if the Pit Bull did catch Kiffo trashing her house then it wouldn't take her more than a microsecond to see my pathetic attempts at distractions for what they were – but even if I did get away with that, I'd be labelled a pervert, a teacher molester. It was a mess, and no mistake. And why? Because of some misguided sense of loyalty, based on the flimsy premise that Kiffo and I shared some history. That there was a bond we were both forced to acknowledge. Stuff it! Kiffo was right. This wasn't any of my concern. I resolved, there and then, to mind my own business in the future. I'd say that the whole thing was an attempt at a joke, a malicious joke intended to embarrass an unpopular teacher.

I knew I'd be in deep trouble. The school authorities didn't take kindly to that type of behaviour, but what else could I do?

I was so deep in thought that I was home before I was aware of it. The Fridge, for once, was waiting for me and offered to heat up some soup, but I didn't feel like talking to anyone, so I made an excuse and went to bed. She looked a little hurt and I guess I could understand why. I was constantly taking the piss out of the fact that she was absent all the time, and when she did get a chance to spend time with me, I could only slink off to bed. It was eight-thirty, for God's sake! But I was tired.

So much for my Friday evening! I fell into a deep but troubled sleep. The Pit Bull's face kept appearing before my eyes, then Slasher and finally Kiffo. What a nightmare. Even Stephen King couldn't have dreamed up a more terrifying trio of ugliness.

I was woken by a scratching sound. I raised myself up in bed groggily and looked at my alarm clock. It was 5.31 in the morning. I put my head back on the pillow and gathered the duvet around me. The sound came again. It wasn't scratching. It was gravel being thrown against my window. I thought I had had my full quota of sinking feelings, but it was with another that I made my way to the window and saw the balaclavaed, camouflaged figure of Kiffo in the front yard.

Chapter 7
Three conversations

| **ONE**
| *Time: 5.35 a.m., Saturday*
| *Location: Calma's front yard*

Bloody hell, Kiffo,' I said. 'What time do you call this?'

Kiffo looked tired and fed up. He shook his head.

'Dunno.'

'Well, at least you're safe. I had visions of you in a police lock-up, spilling your guts. I was half expecting the police to show up. What happened, Kiffo? How did you get out of there?'

Kiffo sat down wearily on the grass.

'I've been in there all night, Calma,' he said. 'I only got out about twenty minutes ago. Came straight here. It was a nightmare.'

I hadn't been feeling too charitable towards Kiffo, as you can probably imagine, but the sight of him melted my resentment. He was trembling slightly and there were large bags under his eyes. He looked on the point of exhaustion. I made him wait outside while I crept back into the dark kitchen and made him a strong cup of coffee. More skulking around. If Mum woke up, she'd throw a fit. I couldn't imagine her being too keen on early morning trysts in the front yard with camouflage-geared persons of dubious moral character. I slipped out the back door, banging my ankle on the door frame and spilling scalding liquid over my hand. Strangling yelps of pain, I forced the cup on to Kiffo. Only when he'd got himself outside of half a cup did he tell me what had happened.

'I didn't hear her come back until it was too late,' he started.

I hadn't wanted to interrupt, but I couldn't help myself.

'What do you mean, you couldn't hear? I was making enough noise outside to register on the Richter scale. The neighbours five doors down came out, for God's sake. You must have heard.'

Kiffo looked a little embarrassed.

'Yeah, well, I'm a little . . . well, deaf. Just in my left ear, you understand.'

'You might have told me this, Kiffo, before you had me as lookout for you. If I'd known that letting off a cannon would have been the only way of attracting your attention, I might have been a little less willing to get myself involved in this mess.'

'What?'

'Never mind. Go on.'

'It was horrible, Calma. I was in her bedroom, checking things out. I hadn't done nothing at that stage. I was wondering whether I should pee over her pet parrot, when I heard her coming up the stairs. I had no time to get away, so I hid in her walk-in wardrobe. It was awful in there. She had all these . . . all these . . . woman things hanging up. You know, underwear things.'

The image of Miss Payne's underwear was not one I wanted to dwell on.

'I had my face stuffed into something lacy with wires, Calma,' he continued, his voice catching with emotion. 'And a cockroach was climbing up the insides of my trousers. The wardrobe was dark and smelly and I could hear her moving round. And then that bloody great dog started to bark. It was in the room with her. I thought that at any moment she would throw open the doors of the wardrobe and the dog would rip my throat out. If I'd known then that I would be spending the next nine hours surrounded by her . . . you know, things . . . I'd probably have been glad if it had.'

'Nine hours! But you must have had some chance to get out of there.'

Kiffo shook his head.

'Nah,' he said. 'There were a good few hours when the Pit Bull was downstairs, but every time I went to open the door that bloody hound kicked up a helluva noise. She got really suspicious. Came upstairs about five or six times to check the place out. I could hear her growling. Her and the bloody dog. Could be relatives, them. The worst bit, though, was when she went to bed.'

Kiffo's face drained of colour and for a moment I thought he wouldn't be able to go on. He looked in need of one of those disaster counsellors they have – you know, for victims of landslides and bushfires. He was about as traumatised by his experiences as anyone could be. To his credit, though, he swallowed and carried on.

'I could hear her undressing, Calma.' His voice shook. 'It was horrible. That must have been about eleven-thirty. And by that time the cockroach was nesting in my bal— trousers and I couldn't move and I wanted to sneeze and I couldn't do that and my nose was really itching where her thingies were hanging against my face and . . .'

'Calm down, Kiffo. You're safe now.'

He took a few deep breaths and swallowed the rest of the coffee. Suppressing the shudders, he carried on in a calmer tone.

'I could hear the bed creak as she got into it. Must be a helluva bed, that one. Reinforced, I reckon. And then, just when I thought it couldn't get no worse . . . it did.'

'Why? What happened?'

'She had a CD player by the bed. I'd checked it out earlier. You know, one of the things I was going to trash. And she put on a CD. For, like, an hour.'

'So what's wrong with that?'

'It was that Irish dickhead. You know, the one who stamps about on stage, feet wiggling all over the place, but the rest of him all stiff like he's got a metal bar up his arse? That one. It was really gross, Calma. All those fiddles and accordions and things. I thought I was going to die.'

I could see his point. It did seem unnecessary torture.

'But what about when she went to sleep? You must have had a chance then.'

'She lets the dog sleep with her. Poor bloody thing. What with her and all the Irish music it has to listen to, you can't blame it for being a vicious bastard. So there was no chance. I tried a few times, when I could hear her snoring, but as soon as I made a move, the dog would do this low growling bit and I'd have to stay dead still. I tell you, standing still for near on nine hours is not something I want to do again in a hurry.'

'Poor Kiffo. It does sound appalling. So how come you got out when you did? Don't tell me she gets up at 5.00 a.m. to go for a ten k run?'

Kiffo brightened.

'It's sorta weird, Calma. Get this. At four-forty-something the phone rings. I damn near crapped myself. I'd kinda fallen asleep on my feet by then and I thought it was a police siren. The cockroach in my trousers started jumping about. Like that Irish idiot. So, I'm wide awake and I can hear the Pit Bull talking. She's really tired, her voice all grumpy at being woken up. "Who the hell is it?" she says, or something like that. And then there's this long silence and then she says, "What, now? It's nearly five in the morning. Can't it wait?" More silence. And then she says, "Let Ravioli deal with it." '

'She's talking about pasta at five in the morning?'

'What?'

'You said "ravioli". '

'Well, it was something like that. Some Italian name. There's more silence and then she says, "All right. I'll be there in fifteen minutes. Don't let him get away from you this time, or you're dead." Something along those lines anyway. So she gets up and leaves the house, taking the bloody dog with her. What is all that about, Calma? I mean, who gets up at five in the morning for secret meetings and what does she mean about not getting away and, "or you're dead"?'

'I've no idea, Kiffo. Business, maybe.'

Kiffo snorted.

'Business? She's a teacher, Calma. What business is she doing at five on a Saturday morning? Comparing exercise books? No, she's up to something. You didn't hear her. She sounded really mean on the phone, like whoever she was going to see was going to regret it. Like, major.'

'She always sounds mean.'

'Not like this. This was serious.'

'So what do you reckon it was?'

Kiffo leaned towards me conspiratorially and lowered his voice. Not that he needed to. There was no one awake within a ten kilometre radius.

'I reckon she's a member of the Mafia.'

I shook my head firmly.

'Kiffo. As you pointed out just now, she's an English teacher in a high school. Just how many Mafia members do you think take on second jobs in the education department? "This Mafia business doesn't seem to be paying very well. I think I'll get a teaching job to enhance my pension." Come on. I mean, there'd be opportunities for drug supplying, I guess, but it's not like she's operating a numbers racket on the oval or offering the canteen protection.'

'Well, I dunno, do I? But I'm going to find out.'

'Kiffo, give it a break. We both had a horrible night last night.' I decided that I wouldn't tell him about my protestations of undying love to Miss Payne. Kiffo's not the kind of person to take the charitable view. He'd give me heaps if he knew. 'Let's just cut our losses. Anyway, you've trashed her place now, so that's it, isn't it? Revenge accomplished.'

A look of sheepishness passed over Kiffo's face.

'You did do it, didn't you, Kiffo?' I said. 'I mean, that's why you went there. That's why you spent hours in her walk-in robe. So you could trash her place when she and the hound left. Don't tell me you left without doing it.'

Kiffo looked pained.

'I forgot,' he said.

Two

Time: 9.00 a.m., Monday
Location: Student Counsellor's office

Mrs Mills: Please make yourself comfortable, Calma. How are you today?

Calma: Fine thanks, Mrs Mills.

Mrs Mills: Anything bothering you?

Calma: Only that I was told to come to your office.

Mrs Mills: It bothers you, coming to see the Student Counsellor, does it?

Calma: No. Well, a bit, I suppose.

Mrs Mills: And why do you think that might be?

Calma: Because it suggests I need counselling, I guess.

Mrs Mills: And do you think that you don't?

Calma: Why is everything you say a question?

Mrs Mills: Do questions worry you, Calma?

Calma: You see what I mean?

Mrs Mills: Why do you think you feel the need to get aggressive when questions are being put to you?

Calma: I'M NOT GETTING AGGRESSIVE.

Mrs Mills: Do you feel upset, Calma?

Silence.

Mrs Mills: Let's get back to the original question, shall we? Do you have any idea why you were asked to see me?

Calma: Well . . . I could have a guess, I suppose. Anything to do with Miss Payne, by any chance?

Mrs Mills: Now why did you think that?

Calma: Because . . . oh, never mind.

Mrs Mills: You think about Miss Payne a lot, do you, Calma?

Calma: No! Well, I mean, yes. But not for the reason you're thinking.

Mrs Mills: And what do you think I'm thinking?

Silence.

Mrs Mills: Tell me about your home life, Calma. Your father left when you were in Year 6. Is that right?

Calma: Yes.

Mrs Mills: And how do you feel about that?

Calma: What do you mean 'how do I feel?' How do you think I feel?

Mrs Mills: It's not how I think you feel that's important, Calma. It's how you think you feel. How do you think you feel?

Calma: I feel deliriously happy, Mrs Mills. I haven't stopped laughing since he walked out on us and went to Sydney with the twenty-year-old barmaid from the Blarney Stone Irish pub.

Mrs Mills: Is that right, Calma?

Calma: No, of course it's not right! I was being ironic!

Mrs Mills: Do you often hide your true feelings by telling . . . untruths?

Calma: It was bloody irony!

Mrs Mills: I can see you're getting upset again. Does the mention of your father always get you upset?

Calma: No.

Mrs Mills: Would you say that you are resentful towards men as a result of your childhood experiences?

Calma: No. I resent my father, that's all. Why are we talking about my father?

Mrs Mills: Are you uncomfortable talking about men?

Silence.

Mrs Mills: Is your mother a strong woman?

Calma: Absolutely. Solid steel and enamel. Rusting a bit on the bottom, but that's to be expected. She's not exactly young any more, let's face it. Well past her guarantee.

Mrs Mills: What do you mean by that, Calma?

Calma: My mother is a refrigerator.

Mrs Mills: What do you mean, a refrigerator?

Calma: It's just a joke, Mrs Mills. I see more of the fridge, that's all. Forget it.

Mrs Mills: Your mother works two jobs, doesn't she? I imagine you don't see too much of her. Do you resent that, Calma?

Calma: I don't know about 'resent'. I'd like to see more of her, naturally, but she works hard to provide for me. She's brought me up by herself, doing two jobs and nothing in the way of child support. It's been really hard for her.

Mrs Mills: You admire strong women, then?

Calma: I admire my mother, even if it's at a distance. She's a strong woman. That doesn't mean I admire all strong women.

Mrs Mills: Do you think Miss Payne is a strong woman?

Calma: I'm not convinced she *is* a woman!

Mrs Mills: That is very interesting. Why do you say that?

Silence.

Mrs Mills: Do you often think about Miss Payne's femininity?

Silence.

Mrs Mills: You told Miss Payne that you loved her, didn't you, Calma?

Calma: No. Yes. No. Well, I did, but I didn't mean it.

Mrs Mills: And you followed her to her house, didn't you?

Calma: No, I didn't follow her. I just knew where she lived, that's all.

Mrs Mills: Do you make it a habit to know where your teachers live?

Calma: No.

Mrs Mills: Do you know where any of your other teachers live, Calma?

Calma: No.

Mrs Mills: Miss Payne said that you were behaving

strangely when you came to her house. That you were talking in a disjointed fashion, quite out of character with your normal level of sophistication. That you were nervous. Would you say that was an accurate description?

Calma: I suppose. But I know what you're thinking. I was nervous, but not because I am madly in love with her. I was nervous because . . .

Mrs Mills: Yes?

Calma: Nothing.

Mrs Mills: So you were nervous, breathing heavily, and then you told her that you loved her. Is that right?

Calma: YES! But I didn't tell her I loved her because I love her! I hate her!

Mrs Mills: It's often said that love and hate are two sides of the same coin, Calma, that there is very little difference between them. What do you say to that?

Calma: Yes, I've heard that, Mrs Mills, and I'd say that it is the single biggest heap of crap ever. It's like saying that there is no difference between heaven and hell, or light and dark, or youth and age, or fish and kangaroos. These things are opposites, Mrs Mills . . . well, fish and kangaroos are not exactly opposites, but you know what I mean. Saying that opposite things are really the same is just lazy. And wrong. A philosophy that only the feeble-minded could accept. When I said that I don't love Miss Payne, I meant that I don't love her. When I said that I hated her, I meant that too. No confusion, no possibility of misinterpretation. I hate her!

Mrs Mills: Do you not think that you might be in denial, Calma?

Calma: Yes, I am in denial. I deny that I love her.

Mrs Mills: So you admit that you're in denial. That's a start, Calma. A very promising start. We haven't time right now to continue this discussion. Under normal circumstances we would remove you from Miss Payne's class immediately, for reasons that you will probably understand. Don't panic. I'm not going to do that. Mainly because we are so understaffed at the moment that there actually isn't another class I could put you into . . .

Calma: Please put me into another class, Mrs Mills!

Mrs Mills: I know that you are worried but you'll just have to be strong, Calma. You have to understand that what you are going through is a very common experience for girls of your age. It's nothing to be ashamed of and it doesn't mean that you are abnormal or anything. Now, back to class with you. We'll probably have a little chat once or twice a week, just to make sure everything is under control, if you know what I mean. You can tell me anything, Calma. Anything at all. And it goes without saying that anything that is said within this room remains entirely confidential. Just between us and these four walls. When you let yourself out, dear, could you tell Rachael Smith to step right on in?

Calma: Yes, Mrs Mills.

THREE
Time: 9.45 a.m., Monday
Location: Science classroom

'Rachael Smith says you're gay, Calma. She says you've got the hots for Miss Payne.'

'Rachael Smith is a lying pig!'

'Calma's got the hots for the Pit Bull, Calma's got the hots for the Pit Bull . . .'

Chapter 8
A reflection upon circumstances, after mature consideration

Bugger.

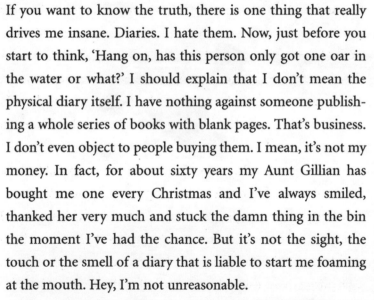

Chapter 9

The cutting edge of educational practice

If you want to know the truth, there is one thing that really drives me insane. Diaries. I hate them. Now, just before you start to think, 'Hang on, has this person only got one oar in the water or what?' I should explain that I don't mean the physical diary itself. I have nothing against someone publishing a whole series of books with blank pages. That's business. I don't even object to people buying them. I mean, it's not my money. In fact, for about sixty years my Aunt Gillian has bought me one every Christmas and I've always smiled, thanked her very much and stuck the damn thing in the bin the moment I've had the chance. But it's not the sight, the touch or the smell of a diary that is liable to start me foaming at the mouth. Hey, I'm not unreasonable.

No. What I hate is the way teachers think that diaries are, in some mysterious fashion, the cutting edge of educational practice. What is it about diaries that excites them so? Do they really think that by setting a diary entry for homework they are somehow tapping into genuine adolescent interests? That we are all going to go, 'Wow, that was one really dull lesson, but now I've got the chance to write a diary entry on it, the adrenalin is really pumping. This is fantastic, inspiring, brilliant . . . oops, I've wet myself with excitement!'? That's only the girls, of course. The boys will, without exception, plan to write *dairy* entries, in which cows, milk and the churning of butter figure prominently. I've a theory about boys and spelling. I think that most of them are born with only half a brian!

And I know the answer to why we are subjected to the mind-numbing routine of diary entries. Laziness. That's what it is. Sheer laziness. And that's something else. 'Use your imagination, class. I want fresh ideas and fresh expression. Now what can I give them to do? I know, I'll trot out that old standby, the diary entry.' Double standards. It makes my blood boil.

I'll tell you another thing. Sometimes – no, probably most times – the diary entry is completely inappropriate. I remember last year our English teacher did *Macbeth* with us. Now I don't know if you know the play but it has this woman, Lady Macbeth, and is she a real cow? This woman is completely evil. She pushes her husband into murdering the king just because she wants to be queen. Initially, he agrees, but later when he says he doesn't think he can do it, she tells him that she would have plucked her own baby from her breast and beaten its brains out, if she had sworn to do it. You know, that nothing would stop her from getting what she wants, even if it means killing her own baby in cold blood. And you believe her! She is one cold, unfeeling woman. So, her husband murders the king and gets the crown and she becomes queen and all. And it's very bloody. Our teacher told us to write a diary entry from the viewpoint of Lady Macbeth after the murder of the old king, who was called Duncan. Can you believe that? This is Shakespeare we are talking about here. High tragedy. And we are expected to imagine that in the middle of all the blood-shed, Lady Macbeth is getting out her Woolies diary every night and jotting a few things down! So this is what I wrote.

Friday, 11.30 p.m.

Dear Diary,

It's been a few nights since I've written to you. I hope I'm not getting lax, but I've been pretty busy recently, what with entertaining the King of Scotland and his three thousand hangers-on. I was all for ordering takeaway, but Macbeth wouldn't have it. He reckons the local Thai restaurant is over-priced and he's been wary of the pizza place ever since he had the seafood thick crust and got crook with food poisoning. So I was up to my elbows in pies and mushy peas for everyone, while Macbeth and old Duncan were watching The Footy Show *and getting a few*

beers down them. Typical bloody men! Anyway, after all
that, Macbeth tells me he doesn't want to murder Duncan
after all. He's changed his mind! I tell you, I gave him
heaps. I was ropeable. I said, 'Listen here, matey, it's just
like when you were supposed to be putting up the shade-
cloth over the pool. That took five bloody months. No way,
mate. Get in there and kill the old bastard right now or
you can forget all about going to the V8 Supercars next
week!' 'Aw, jeez, Lady Mac,' he said. 'Give me a break, will
yer?' To cut a long story short, he does it. Not without a lot
of whingeing and whining, mind. And there is, like, loads
of blood all over the good duvet. Took me hours to get the
stains out. Forget that old stuff about salt being the busi-
ness for stains. Might work for wine, but gobs of blood is a
different matter. By the time I finished, I was completely
knackered. So I'll make this short. To be honest, after the
day I've had, I just fancy a mug of cocoa and a quick read
of Woman's Own. *I'll write again tomorrow, I swear.*

I was expecting a detention for that. I *wanted* a detention!
But do you know what happened? I got a big tick and a B grade.
She hadn't even read it. Sometimes teachers make me sick.

Look, sorry about all this. I know I'm rambling. It's just
that I had a hard time after Rachael Smith had finished
spreading the hot news about my supposed love affair with
the Pit Bull. Not content with telling the entire school within

twenty-five minutes – not a bad effort when there are over eight hundred kids at the school – she then gave the full rundown to the parents, siblings, aunts, uncles, second cousins twice-removed, neighbours, casual acquaintances, newspaper-delivery kids and the bag lady who spends her time gibbering and drooling in the city centre. I'm surprised she didn't take out a full-page advertisement in the local paper. I couldn't watch *60 Minutes* for months afterwards without worrying that my face would appear accompanied by a breathy voice-over, 'Pervert Student Stalks Kindly Teacher.'

[**Rachael Smith – Virgo** in conjunction with Uranus. There is a tendency today to speak without thinking, possibly because you have the brains of a brick. Beware of large-breasted, bespectacled females bearing two-metre lengths of plumbers' piping.]

I don't know if you have ever been in a similar situation. Unlikely, I guess, unless you are, like me, gifted with a talent for inviting disaster. But it's hell. Yeah, OK. I know what you are thinking. 'It'll pass. Worse things happen at sea. Bit of teasing never hurt anyone.' Was that what you were thinking? If it was, please go at once and stick your head in a large bucket of bleach. I know all about treating misfortune with dignity. In theory. But in practice, you wish you were dead. Everywhere I went, there was giggling and immature remarks. Girls would leave the toilets if I went in. I was pathetically grateful that Vanessa still sat next to me in class. She continued to wear boredom like a badge, but there was a subtle change in her attitude. Difficult to be specific. Little things, like the way her body was slightly more closed, as if she was desperate that our legs wouldn't touch under the desk. Maybe it was my imagination, but I thought that even the teachers looked at me slightly differently.

I went straight home from school that day. To be honest, I needed my mum. I wanted to talk things through with her, the way they do on soap operas. You know. All that stuff where the girl says, 'Mum, I'm pregnant by the local heroin addict, my best friend's topped herself and the police want to interview me in connection with the arson at the high school.' And the mum strokes the girl's hair and says, 'It's OK, Charlene, you know that I'll always be here for you.' I needed that kind of thing.

Of course, Mum wasn't back from work and the fridge was, as always, strong, silent and dependable, but rather weak in the empathy stakes. So I kicked it a few times, leaving a couple of decent dents, and I felt a bit better. Then I ate the last of the ice-cream. I didn't particularly feel like it, but it was Mum's favourite and she often had a bowl between shifts, so I forced it down. Pathetic, I know, but someone had to pay.

Overdosed on raspberry ripple, I wandered off to Kiffo's place. Funnily enough, I'd never actually been to his house before, but I knew where he lived. It was not the kind of neighbourhood that you tended to go into if you could avoid it. Particularly when it was getting dark. Particularly if you were a woman. Particularly if you were a woman with huge boobs. What the hell. I didn't care. I think in my state of mind I'd have been more than a match for any roving gang of hoons.

I knocked on the door, and after a few moments Kiffo opened it. He looked at me with surprise and then nodded for me to come in. The front room was a disgrace. I've seen some messes in my time – hell, I've created my fair share – but this took the whole packet of biscuits. Crumpled beer cans were scattered around the carpet, if anything so threadbare and filthy could be dignified with such a name. Old pizza cartons, at least three of them, were also arranged artistically on the floor. Two still contained traces of pizza, though they were clearly so old that any positive identification would have taxed the expertise of the most distinguished forensic scientist. I guessed at thin crust mould with extra botulism topping. The place stank of old socks, sweat, tobacco and despair. Kiffo noticed my expression.

'Yeah, well,' he said. 'It's the cleaning lady's day off. Come in and sit down.'

I looked around. There was nowhere really that I considered a safe place to sit. The couch would have been rejected by the local dump on the grounds that it would have brought down the ambience of the place. Not that I cared too much about the fact that it was held together with fishing wire, or that it sagged alarmingly in strange places, like a depressed storm cloud. But there were things living in it. I could see them moving. It created a strange effect, like those lava lamps. There was a never-ending rearrangement of the pattern. A microbiologist would have been enchanted, but I wasn't sticking my bum anywhere near it. I found a broken bar stool in the corner. It wasn't clean, but at least it wasn't creating its own visible ecosystem. Kiffo slumped into the couch, which gave off a dense cloud of irritated bugs, some, undoubtedly, unknown to modern science.

'Wassup, Calma?' he said, fishing into his pocket and producing a rollie with a distinct dogleg to it.

'You don't want to know, Kiffo,' I said.

'OK,' he replied and lit up. There was a silence.

'Well, when I say you don't want to know, I mean that you probably do want to know. It's kind of a rhetorical question – well, not a question, obviously, more of a rhetorical statement – but it produces a similar effect. You're supposed to press me and then I reveal all. So not at all like a rhetorical statement, when it comes down to it.'

Kiffo narrowed his eyes at me through the cloud of smoke and airborne bacilli.

'You're talking like an English teacher,' he said. 'Don't. It makes me want to throw up. If you've got something to say, then say it.'

Good advice, let's be honest. So I told him all about what I had said to the Pit Bull the night of the break-in and how she'd told the school counsellor –

[Mrs Mills – Gemini. Your normal sense of discretion will desert you today. Beware of unfortunate slips of the tongue caused by either a momentary lapse of concentration or an innate tendency towards verbal diarrhoea.]

– who'd obviously said something to Rachael Spit-In-Her-Eye Smith, who'd let her mouth off the leash and created havoc. As I was telling him, I could feel the tears welling. But I kept them back. Kiffo's one of those guys who doesn't like crying. It would embarrass him and he wouldn't know what to do. So he'd have to get angry. Still, I tried to tell him how I felt as if my whole life had been ripped up and thrown away in the course of a single afternoon. I wanted him to know that this was important.

And he listened. When I had done with the tale, a little breathless with the effort of keeping emotion out of it, he threw his cigarette on to the carpet and ground it out with his heel. Then he leaned back and looked at me.

'You, Calma,' he said, 'are something else.'

'Yeah, I know.'

'You did that for me? You told the Pit Bull you loved her just to give me more time? I don't know what to say. I really don't. No one has never done nothing like that for me. Never.'

'Never done *anything* like that,' I corrected.

'But you *did*, Calma. You did.'

'Listen. It was just a spur-of-the-moment thing, you know. It doesn't mean we're engaged or anything. Anyway, that's all beside the point. My life has just been flushed down the toilet because of it and I don't know what to do!'

Kiffo fished out another cigarette.

'Don't do nothing,' he said.

'What do you mean?'

Kiffo leaned forward and jabbed his cigarette at me like an accusing finger.

'Christ, Calma. You're supposed to be the big brains of the class, but you're a dumb shit at times. What *can* you do? Go around saying to everyone, "Listen, I'm not a lesbo, swear to God." You think that'll stop people talking?'

'No, but . . .'

'Stuff 'em. I've spent my whole life dealing with people who think I'm a step below a cockroach. Do I let that worry me? Hell, I am what I am. I don't look for people's approval and you shouldn't neither. What you did for me was real good, a real nice thing to do.'

'Thanks, but . . .'

'If it's caused other people to think bad of you, well, that's their problem, not yours. At least two of us know the truth about you and the Pit Bull. The rest can shove it.'

This was, by some considerable margin, the longest speech I had ever heard from Kiffo. I wasn't used to being talked over by someone whose preferred mode of communication was an occasional grunt, normally accompanied by offensive body language. I felt touched that my predicament had moved him to that extent. What's more, he was right. There wasn't anything I could do, but just ignoring the situation didn't seem too appealing either. For all that, what he said was important to me, particularly the bit about the two of us knowing the truth.

'You *don't* fancy her, do you?' he added.

'Christ, Kiffo!'

'Sorry. Just checking.'

We sat for a while, lost in our own thoughts. Talking to Kiffo had done me good, just like always. It had taken my mind off my own problems a bit, which was ironic, really, since that was all we had been talking about. Maybe it was something to do with the surroundings, the evidence of Kiffo's bleak existence. I mean, the room *was* disgusting. I'll say that for the Fridge. She might be working every waking hour, but she still has the time and the energy to keep the house pretty tidy. But Kiffo and his dad? It was a different world they lived in, a world where normal standards didn't apply – exactly, I suppose, the kind of world that the Fridge didn't want for me. I mulled that over for a while. I could see what she wanted to achieve. I just couldn't tell whether it was worth the price we were paying to achieve it. Gives you a headache, thinking about stuff like that, so I stopped.

Anyway, my eye had been caught by a framed photograph on the wall. It was of a young man in his late teens, leaning against a wall. He was smiling broadly, as if in response to something said as the shutter was clicking. Whatever that might have been was gone, the words long since evaporated, but the reaction was still there, frozen in that grin. He looked happy, full of life, energy radiating from the posture, the narrowed eyes, the red hair spiked into crazy angles. The glass of the photograph gleamed. There was not a mark on it, or on the frame, which had obviously been polished recently. It was a small oasis of cleanliness against the stained backdrop of the wall.

I glanced over at Kiffo. He was looking at me, his expression neutral.

'Kiffo, look—'

'Time to go home, Calma,' he interrupted. 'We wouldn't want you to catch anything life-threatening here, now would we? I'll walk you back.'

It doesn't do to argue with Kiffo. I got up from the stool and checked myself for alien life-forms while Kiffo rolled another cigarette and opened the door for me. We walked for a while in silence. The street lights around his place were all out, probably smashed by those in his area who preferred darkness as a business environment. In other circumstances, I would have found it frightening, but Kiffo's presence was reassuring. I looked up at the sky. The stars were hammered into its blackness like small, bright nails. I wanted to talk about the photograph, but didn't know how to start. I guess I didn't have the courage.

'Kiffo?' I said.

'What?'

'If I ask you something, will you answer me honestly?'

'Depends.'

'Why do you try so hard to give the impression that you're dumb?'

'I am dumb.'

'No.' I stopped. This was important and I wanted an answer. 'You're not. And you know it. All that stuff you were telling me back at your place, about looking for people's approval. That's not the kind of thing a dumb person would be saying. So why pretend?'

He shrugged, like the topic of conversation was boring him.

'I'm not pretending to be anything, Calma. I'm me, that's all. Like I was saying earlier. Other people think it's dumb, what I am. Who cares?'

'Does it matter what I think about you?'

Kiffo took a deep draw on his cigarette and thought

for a moment.

'Yeah,' he said. 'It does. But then, you don't think I'm dumb, do you? So no worries.'

'But it *is* important what other people think about you, Kiffo. It *is* important if they think you are stupid when you're not!'

'Why?'

'It just is.' I was floundering and I knew it.

'I'll tell you what's important, Calma.'

'What?'

'What we do about the Pit Bull. That's important. Where do we go from here?'

'Are you crazy?' I said. 'We do nothing about the Pit Bull. I've already had enough trouble with that woman. I'm going to keep my head down, do the assignments she sets and hope that she'll either leave soon or get run over by a very large road train. Preferably the latter.'

'Yeah. You're right,' he said, scratching behind his ear. 'It's too dangerous. Keep your head down. That's the way to go. You're right.'

That stopped me. God, he can be a real bastard at times.

'Now, hang on a moment, Kiffo,' I said. I think I even put my hands on my hips. 'Just because I'm right, doesn't mean I'm right, you know.'

'Hey, you got me with that one, Calma. Just too smart for me, I guess.'

'Cut it out, Kiffo. Don't think, not even for one minute, that you are going to do anything about the Pit Bull without me. OK?'

'But you just said . . .'

'Never mind what I just said. We are in this together.'

I meant it too. It hit me, right then, with all the force of a genuine revelation, that I only took chances verbally. Quick at shooting from the lip, but a bit of a wimp when it came to anything else. Maybe old Kiffo, all action and adrenalin, would make a good partner, a Clyde to my Bonnie, a Butch Cassidy to my Sundance. I decided not to share this with Kiffo. I don't think he would have liked it if I'd called him 'Butch'. But what the hell? I'd come this far and like old Macbeth said: 'I am stepped in blood so far that to go back is as tedious as to go o'er.' Or something like that. And anyway, I was going to find out about the connection between the Pit Bull and Kiffo, regardless of what he might think.

We got back to my place and I invited him in for a cup of coffee.

'Thanks, but I'd better get back,' he said. 'Dad'll be home soon, full of grog and wanting dinner. If it's not ready for him, there'll be trouble.'

I watched as he walked off into the dark, a slight, bandy-legged figure, hunched and curiously vulnerable. I had little first-hand knowledge of the kind of life he led, but I knew that it was loveless and full of casual cruelty. I felt even closer to him then than normal. Not the sort of closeness you feel for the underprivileged, when your own comfortable existence is held up to theirs. Not the sort that is tinged with guilt. I just felt – and I know this sounds really obvious and almost childish – that we were both here and human. That for all our differences, we were still, like the rest of humanity, ninety-nine per cent indistinguishable from each other.

Never mind that the bastard was lying to me.

The Fridge was in bed when I went in. I had a hot shower and snuggled under the duvet, the aircon blasting above my head. It felt great, the contrast between the artificial chill in the air and the sense of womb-like security in bed. I dozed a little and thought about the day. Curiously, I didn't feel half so bad now. What had seemed a nightmare was only a bad dream and fading with every passing moment. I thought about Kiffo's back as he walked off into the night, and the sense of security that gave. Most of all, I curled myself around an image of someone, carefully, lovingly, cleaning a photograph of a grinning young man.

Yes, it had been a strange day. As I slipped under the surface of sleep, I was bothered by just one thought. I felt somehow that it was important to write down everything I was feeling, to record my thoughts in case they appeared stupid in the morning. Or, even worse, cloudy and insubstantial.

Sometimes diaries are a really good idea, you know. It was a shame I'd thrown so many away.

MARCH: Primary School, Year 6.

You are pinned up against the school fence. You're scared, but try not to show it. As you look up into the boy's face, your eyes blink nervously behind large, multicoloured glasses. He is taller than you and a lot heavier. He has a stupid face, leaden and cruel. As he leans towards you, he prods you painfully in the shoulder with a blunt, dirty finger.

'You need to watch your mouth,' he says. 'You think you can say what you like about me, is that it? You think I won't hit a girl?'

He pushes his face further into yours and you can smell stale tobacco. His face buckles into anger as you say nothing. His right hand, cocked behind his shoulder, clenches into a fist. You close your eyes and wait.

Chapter 10

Every dog has its night

FBI Special Agent Calma Harrison stepped from the shower. She got dressed quickly, paying no attention to the thin scar that ran down the side of her stomach. A memento of a fight in Beirut. Just before she had broken his neck, he had slashed her across the abdomen. Later, she had stitched herself with a sharpened twig and a length of twine she had fashioned from local native grasses. A neat job, even more remarkable because she had no anaesthetic. She preferred to bite on a bullet. One time, she had been sewing her ear back on in Botswana when she bit too hard and shot a passing antelope.

Her eyes flickered as she detected a sound in the corridor outside her hotel room. Nerves on full alert, she whipped her Walther PPK semi-automatic from the holster and with cat-like grace backflipped across the room, pressing herself against the wall. There was a knock on the door.

'Who is it?' she breathed.

'Room Service,' came the reply.

Calma registered the voice and instantaneously processed its accent. Despite the attempt at disguise — good, but not quite good enough — she placed it within a second. A rarely heard dialect from the East Bank of the Mezzanine Strip. A tiny village called B'Gurrup. The owner of the voice lived three streets down from the butcher's shop. Maybe four, Calma thought. She hadn't been to B'Gurrup in over fifteen years.

Her mind raced. Who had connections with the Mezzanine Strip? It was a filthy, dangerous place, a hotbed of mercenaries, hit men and used-car salesmen. The answer was clear. Only one person would think of employing the specialist skills to be found in B'Gurrup. Her arch enemy. The Pit Bull.

Calma did a forward roll and in less than three seconds, two hundred rounds from the Walther crashed through the spy hole in the centre of the massive oak door. She opened the door and examined the bloody mess on the doorstep. The would-be assassin had a small ground-to-ground heat-seeking missile-launcher in his right hand. In his left was a Kalashnikov rifle, a cluster grenade and a Swiss Army knife. This man had come prepared for action.

'Too bad, buddy,' Calma growled as she stepped over him and headed for the elevator. Curiously, she felt a sense of relief. She still remembered that incident in Miami when she had accidentally blown away the night manager of her hotel. She had been certain that his accent was from a small Shiite community that had ordered her death through a high-level fatwa. It turned out that he had simply had a bad head cold.

Calma stepped from the hotel on to the bustling streets. Kiffing was waiting for her at the agreed park bench, idly kicking a small Pekingese dog that was trying to attach itself to his trouser leg.

'News?' said Calma.

'The Pit Bull is here. We're not sure why, but we think it might be connected to next week's UN Assembly. The word on the street is that there is to be an assassination attempt on a major world figure. As you know, Harrison, the presence of the Pit Bull can only mean one thing. Terror and devastation.'

'That's two things,' said Calma.

'OK, then. Two things,' said Kiffing.

'You want me to take her out?' asked Calma.

'Won't that make her suspicious? A date with a complete stranger?'

'No. I mean, kill her.'

'That's a negative. We want her alive.'

Calma thought quickly. She mentally replayed all the information she had gleaned about the Pit Bull. Simultaneously, she analysed the Spassky/Fischer sixth game of the 1972 World Chess Championship, finding an

Enigma Variation that poor Boris had overlooked in the end game. It was a form of mental gymnastics that helped her focus. She turned to Kiffing.

'Any idea of her whereabouts?'

'We have a deep throat in Mossad. The word is that she'll stake out the pre-Assembly shindig taking place at the Hilton tonight.'

That made sense. The trouble was that the Pit Bull was an expert in disguise. Calma remembered the assassination of an African leader the previous year. It bore all the hallmarks of the Pit Bull's work. Yet one eyewitness swore that the killer was actually a small bull mastiff.

'I'll be there,' she said, 'but I want full back-up. I'll need an OP35 with an APB, complete tactical support, a digitised micro-cam with satellite link-up, solar-powered Kevlar vest with drop sides and EVA capability. Is that clear?'

'Well...not entirely affirmative, now you come to mention it.'

'Just do it, Kiffing. We are not dealing with amateurs here.'

Later that evening Calma Harrison, disguised as a balding oriental dwarf, surveyed the exterior of the Hilton. She was pressed up against a tree in the extensive grounds and her camouflage make-up ensured that from a distance she merely looked like a piece of flaking bark. Patting the bulge of the Walther PPK, she settled down to wait, the trunk of the tree pressing a little uncomfortably into her back...

'Wake up, for God's sake, Calma.'

The voice seemed to be coming from a long way off. I opened my eyes slowly. Surely it wasn't morning already? The first thing I saw was Kiffo's face about two centimetres from mine. Imagine waking up and finding yourself staring at the Phantom of the Opera without his mask at close range, and you'll have some idea of the kind of shock I got.

'Bloody hell, Kiffo,' I yelled. 'Don't do that to me!'

'Shut up!'

I raised my head and it all came back. Kiffo's stupid idea of staking out the Pit Bull's house again, on the off chance that she'd be doing another of her early morning assignations. A real stab in the dark. Which is exactly what I felt like giving Kiffo at that precise moment. Obviously I had dozed off. My shoulder was hurting from where I had been pressing up against a knot in the tree. My right leg had pins and needles. That bloody casuarina tree again. The same one I had waited under for Kiffo on the night of my declaration of undying love. I was beginning to bond with that tree, I can tell you. Maybe the Drama lessons hadn't been a complete waste of time, after all. 'Feel yourself *becoming* the tree, Calma. Feel the sap rising.'

I struggled to my feet, catching at a cramp in my left thigh where the sap was obviously having difficulty getting through.

'What time is it?'

'About three-thirty.'

It took a moment to register.

'Are you out of your tiny mind? But of course you are. Stupid question. Three-thirty? Three-thirty? If I'd known we were going to be out this late I'd have brought a camping stove and a portable TV.'

'Oh, stop moaning, Calma. There's no point going home at ten o'clock, is there? I mean, when she goes out on one of these meetings, it's in the early hours of the morning, isn't it?'

'Hang on, Kiffo. You're talking as if this is some sort of regular occurrence, like the orbit of Uranus or something. You've only seen her go out once. Doesn't mean she makes a habit of it or anything.'

'I've got a feeling about tonight, OK?'

'So you're clairvoyant now, are you?'

'Give it a break, willya?'

'I can tell you exactly what is going to happen, Kiffo,' I said. 'Absolutely bugger all, that's what. We are going to sit here under this stupid casuarina until dawn and then we are going to go home, get dressed for school, go into her class and prop our eyelids open with matchsticks. And she is going to be even more horrible to us than normal on the grounds that sleeping through her lesson is absolutely forbidden, on pain of death, and then—'

But I never got to finish. The Pit Bull's front door opened and that familiar, threatening bulk was now approaching the front gate. I pressed myself further back into the tree. Would I ever get the imprint of bark out of my back? There was a snuffling sound and I could just make out the heaving mass of Slasher. The night was profoundly dark. Just as well, I suppose. The Pit Bull and Slasher made odd lumps of darker blackness against the night, grisly silhouettes that moved like one being. It was creepy. Kiffo leaned closer to me and we watched silently as Miss Payne made a right turn out of the gate and moved silently down the road. I became aware that I was holding my breath. Kiffo leaned in closer and whispered into my ear.

'You were saying, Calma smarty pants?'

'Where the hell is she going at three-thirty in the morning?' I gasped.

To be perfectly honest, I had taken Kiffo's story with a small pinch of salt. Well, a bloody great handful, in fact. It wasn't that I didn't believe him, exactly. I just thought that maybe he had embroidered things a little. You know, the mysterious phone conversation, leaving the house. I'd figured that maybe she had got up in the night and he had taken the opportunity to get the hell out of there while the going was good. And the rest would have been just a bit of macho stuff. Making a big deal out of what had been a humiliating experience. I wanted to apologise to Kiffo but now didn't seem the right time.

'I told you, Calma,' he said, a note of triumph in his voice. 'Maybe once you could explain away. But who in their right mind keeps on going out in the middle of the night, particularly when they've got a job to go to? I tell you, she is up to no good. And we have to find out what it is. Come on.'

Now I know I have given the impression that I was getting a little tired of that casuarina tree. But I can tell you, when the time came to leave, it had never seemed more attractive. It's one thing to hang around outside someone's house, but quite another to follow them down deserted streets at some godforsaken time in the morning. But I had no opportunity to voice my misgivings to Kiffo. He was off like a rat up a drainpipe and I had no option but to follow him. I didn't fancy trailing the Pit Bull, but neither did I fancy hiding under a tree, alone, at that time of night.

Let me tell you something. In the movies, following a person looks like the easiest thing in the world. All you do is walk a discreet distance behind. When they turn around you feign interest in the shop window of an oriental emporium or something. It isn't like that in real life. OK, I know the circumstances were somewhat different. For one thing, there wasn't an oriental emporium within ten kilometres. But the main thing was that there was very little cover. I mean, if the Pit Bull turned around, there we'd be, frozen under a street-lamp. Difficult to explain away as a casual late night jog. Kiffo and I zigzagged from one side of the road to the other, moving from bush to bush, crouching behind the odd parked car. But for a lot of the time we were out in the open. It's a horrible feeling to know that just one backwards glance would be enough to pin you in a metaphorical spotlight.

Problem number two. It's quiet at night. Unbelievably quiet. Even the night insects seemed to have taken a vow of silence. So we couldn't stay too close on her heels for fear that either she or the evil hound, Slasher, would hear our footsteps. That didn't bother me, mind. I'd have been happy with a fair distance. Something like twenty-five kilometres, for example. But it did make it difficult to keep her in view. When she turned a corner, we'd run like hell, keeping on the grass verge to deaden the sound. It was OK for Kiffo – he didn't have to keep a protective arm across his boobs. I was running flat out, and mine threatened to knock my glasses off.

Problem three. When we reached a corner, we had to peer round very carefully. For all we knew, she could have been a metre or two away and a couple of peering, sweaty, dis-embodied faces might just conceivably have drawn a little unwanted attention. This meant that all the time we made up on the mad sprint was lost on gingerly peering around the next corner. God, it was a nightmare. Once, we turned a corner and there was no sign of her at all. A couple of roads radiated off and she could have taken any one of them. So we had to take a chance and run to the point where we could get a good view in every direction. As luck would have it, we spotted the pooch's backside as it turned yet another corner.

Finally, we came to a large intersection. This time, though, we could hear voices. Kiffo and I crouched down and very carefully looked around the corner. About ten metres down the road, the Pit Bull was talking to a man. They were standing under a streetlight and we had a clear view of them. The man was small, thin-lipped and bloodless. Like a ferret. He reminded me of the little guy you used to see in gangster movies. You know, the one who was always next to Robert De Niro, the one who was completely off his head and liable to shoot someone in the groin if he didn't like the look of them. The runt of the litter, but mean as anything.

They were having an animated conversation, two sets of arms flapping all over the place, though we couldn't make out the actual words. It was a residential street, but they were outside a large hall, a likely meeting place for Scouts or other paramilitary organisations. You know the sort of thing. The man was jangling a bunch of keys. After a few more moments of semaphore practice, he unlocked the door of the hall and they disappeared inside. A few seconds later, a light came on. I glanced at Kiffo, raised my eyebrows and he gave me a quick nod. Having come this far, there was no way we were prepared to give up now.

Kiffo and I padded around the side of the building, looking for a convenient window, the kind that in movies are invariably positioned to afford maximum spying potential. It soon became obvious that the builder of this place had wilfully ignored this architectural necessity. The only window likely to offer any view was impractically positioned about two and a half metres above the ground. A possibility if you were a member of the Australian basketball team, but not a great deal of use to us. Fortunately, a quick exploration of the grounds revealed a number of milk crates and we piled these up in a rough pyramid underneath the window. It didn't look particularly safe but unless we stumbled across a cherry picker in the undergrowth it was going to have to do. Kiffo and I climbed gingerly up the crates, stopping every few moments to sway gently as the whole arrangement shifted under our weight. Finally we were able to grab hold of the windowsill and peer into the room.

I'm not the most house-proud person in the world, but that window was a disgrace. The accumulated filth of two millennia seemed ingrained into its surface. Nonetheless, we could just about see the runt and the Pit Bull sitting at a table. Or rather, we could see the Pit Bull pretty clearly, old Slasher sitting at her side, but only the disembodied arms of the runt. There was a document case on the table in front of them.

I had to admit that it all looked like very funny business. Why would you need to meet someone at that time of night? What could possibly be so important that the telephone wouldn't do? Why would a small spider choose just this moment to go for a pre-dawn amble across my cheek? Weighty questions, indeed. And then, just as the tickling on my cheek was reaching unbearable proportions, the runt reached across the table and undid the document case. He pulled out a small bag and dropped it in front of the Pit Bull. I felt Kiffo's hand tighten on my arm. The Pit Bull reached out and for one fleeting moment I caught a glimpse of white powder before she took the bag and shoved it in her coat pocket. Yet more questions raced through my mind. Could the contents of the bag really be drugs? Could we really be witnessing what is known in all the best movies as a 'drop'? Could this really be a sneeze building at the back of my nose?

At least I got the answer to the last question. It was. And it was one of those unstoppable ones, the kind that if you try to contain it with your hand or something, it'll blow the back of your head off. I have to confess that when it arrived, it did so with maximum decibels. I don't know who was most surprised: me, Kiffo, the spider or the trio inside the hall. At least I had about one tenth of a second warning. For Kiffo, it must have been like a shotgun going off in his ear. He leaped about three metres in the air, his face twisted into an expression that, under other circumstances, would have been quite comical, and the whole flimsy structure we were standing on collapsed in a crash of cascading plastic.

'Sorry,' I said, after we had landed in a tangle on the ground. Kiffo turned a disbelieving face in my direction.

'Better out than in,' I added.

Maybe he would have hit me. I wouldn't have blamed him. There wasn't a chance, though. We heard a startled gasp, the unmistakable sound of a door being opened hurriedly, a large dog tearing at the ground with its claws and the rattle of a chain clasp being released. Slasher had been building up a fair bit of momentum while on the leash. Like one of those old wind-up cars. You'd rev the wheels against the floor and when you released it, the car would zoom off at about two hundred kilometres an hour and smash your mum's prize vase in the corner of the living room. Well, old Slash was clearly a bit like that. We could hear the thud of giant paws crashing against the ground. It sounded like a Sherman tank was coming towards us.

'Run!' yelled Kiffo, a little unnecessarily. I already had a twenty-metre head start on him.

Have you ever seen those films where they use a hand-held

camera during action sequences? Everything jumps around and all you can hear is the sound of heavy breathing? Think of that and you will get some idea of the next few minutes. I had never run so fast. The only thing that crossed my mind was whether it was possible to get whiplash in the mammaries. Head up, arms and legs pumping. I'd have amazed my PE teacher. If an athletics scout had been around, I'd probably have made the national squad for the one hundred metres. But whatever I did, I couldn't shake the dog. I could hear it pounding along behind me, the sound of its harsh breathing getting closer by the second. I had no idea what had happened to Kiffo. Under the circumstances, I could only worry about myself.

Just when I felt that the damn thing was about to clasp its yellowing teeth around my ankle I did a sort of sideways leap over a low fence bordering someone's property. The dog attempted to change direction too, and I heard it smash into the metal chain link. I had an image of its face being squeezed into about six separate diamond shapes – you know, like in those cartoons where the cat gets sliced up into segments. It gave me a few precious seconds though. I ran straight across the yard, dodging the odd palm tree that suddenly loomed up at me in the dark. It wasn't enough. Old Slasher had obviously had lessons in fence hurdling because all too soon I could hear the sound of his breathing closing in again. He sounded pissed off as well. Trust me, you can tell these things when you are being pursued by a creature whose sole raison d'être is to supplement its normal diet with human rump steak.

Even a massive burst of adrenalin wears off pretty quickly. I was tiring and I knew it. Just when I felt that it was all over, that, frankly, I couldn't be bothered any more, a sort of miracle happened. One moment I was running over grass and the next a dark mass appeared at my feet. Before I had time to even think about it, I jumped and cleared an in-ground spa by about two metres. Slasher wasn't quite so lucky, though. I could hear a huge splash as he dived straight in. Must have been quite a surprise. One moment he's got the scent of blood in his nostrils and the next he's doing the breaststroke. Mind you, the size and sheer bulk of the hound might have drained the pool for all I knew.

For a while, though, I had clear space behind me. I summoned the last of my fading strength and made for the fence at the rear of the yard. This fence was much higher. Perhaps the security-conscious owners had decided that if they could only afford decent perimeter fencing on one side, they'd put it at the back. This was one serious fence.

I threw myself at it and scrambled up the chain link. Even with my momentum I was still a way from the top and I had to scrabble with my feet for purchase. Then I heard it. The unmistakable sound of a very wet, seriously pissed off dog making a final lunge for its quarry. I guess it thought that it was game over. There I was with my arse wriggling at a tempting and achievable height. I could feel it launching itself like an Exocet missile.

It was then that I felt a strong hand grip my wrist and pull me forcefully up the fence. I had no time to register what was going on before a sharp pain shot through my left foot. Slasher had finally made contact. Bear in mind that this was one heavy dog. Remember also that I'm hanging from a chain link fence with this dog attached to me like a plumb line. Looking up, I could see Kiffo's face, red with strain as he tried to lift me to safety. I knew what it was like to be the rope in the middle of a tug of war. For a while, I thought Slasher would win. The veins were standing out in Kiffo's neck like hot dog sausages. The next moment my shoe came loose and the dog plummeted to the ground with a satisfying thud. The weight gone from my leg, I soared over the top of the fence, adding high jump expertise to my new-found sprinting talent.

Kiffo and I lay in a heap on the other side of the fence. Slasher, enraged beyond endurance, threw himself at the links. I took a good look into his eyes. Believe me, he was not in a charitable mood. This was not a dog that was inclined to forgive and forget. But he was also a powerless dog. The fence was too high.

Kiffo and I scrambled to our feet and took off into the darkness. We had no idea if there was a hole somewhere that Slasher could slink through, or if the owners of the property, woken by the hellish racket that the dog was now making, would not appear with sawn-off shotguns. Anyway, we needed to be as far away from there as possible.

Twenty minutes later we arrived at my house. It was only then that I realised how badly my foot was hurting. Kiffo and I didn't talk much. We were both too exhausted to spend any time with words. He just loped off into the darkness and I let myself in. Luckily, the Fridge was asleep. I had left the house via my bedroom window at about nine-thirty that evening and she had obviously found no reason to disturb what she must have thought was her sleeping daughter.

I bathed my foot in antiseptic and put some plasters on it. I had read somewhere that a dog bite carried all sorts of nasty germs, that you should get a rabies shot, but under the circumstances I decided to trust to luck. My foot wasn't as badly cut as I had thought at first. It would probably swell and bruise, but apart from one rather nasty puncture mark, I had gotten off lightly.

The only problem was my shoe. Slasher still had it. A red Converse. Distinctive. Physical evidence linking me to the scene of the crime. But I was too tired to worry unduly about it. I put its mate securely in the bottom of my wardrobe, sank into bed without bothering to shower, and was instantly submerged in a dreamless sleep.

You wait for the fist to land but nothing happens.
You open your eyes. The boy's hand is still cocked,
but is covered by another. The fat boy's head is
turned to one side, surprise, like a stain, over his
plump features. He looks at the other boy – a boy
with red hair and cold eyes. They stand for a while,
staring, sizing each other up, hands locked
together in unlikely intimacy. The red-haired boy
is smaller by far, yet he seems big somehow. The
silence is like a tight thread.

'Leave her alone,' says the boy with red hair.

His voice is so calm it scares you more than the
fist poised above you. The heavy boy licks his lips
nervously. He is weighing his chances. But it's not
the physical threat. The two are hopelessly mis-
matched in terms of weight and physique. It's in the
eyes. The sense that body size is unimportant compared to strength of will. His eyes slide away as
if looking for escape. Finally he shrugs the
restraining hand away.

'Ah, she's not worth it, anyway,' he says and
walks off. He seems smaller somehow. You look at the
red-haired boy.

'Thanks,' you say.

The boy looks at you and he is difficult to read.

'Fuck off,' he says, without malice.

Chapter 11

Cinderella complex

In the morning, my foot had swollen to the size of a watermelon. I woke up and the first thing I was aware of was a pulsing pain, as if someone was rhythmically beating the sole of my foot with a large piece of bamboo. I carefully removed the bed sheet. To be honest, I was a bit worried that my whole leg had dropped off in the middle of the night and that I was suffering from those phantom pains that amputees experience. When I saw my foot, I actually wished it had dropped off. Hanging from the end of my ankle was a bruised pulp, like a gigantic and over-ripe plum. It was as if someone had carefully inflated a very large cane toad, spray-painted it inexpertly with the primary colours and then attached it with liquid nails to the end of my leg. It was a mess.

I tried walking. That was fine until I put weight on it and the bolt of pain threatened to lift my entire brain pan from the cerebral cortex. So I tried favouring my right foot. That was OK for a while. With practice, I developed a shuffling gait that made me look like an extra in a B-grade zombie movie. Or, I could have put a hump on my back and I would have been a dead ringer for Quasimodo.

Next problem. The obvious thing would have been for me to take the day off school. That would have been easy. I could hear the Fridge downstairs making coffee and coughing over the first cigarette of the day. All it required was a halfway convincing display of stomach pains, the odd heart-rending groan, and I would have been home and dry. The trouble was I *wanted* to go to school. I wanted to talk to Kiffo. We had shared an adventure and there is nothing worse than not being able to replay all the details with someone who had been through it with you. The other thing was I wanted to see the reaction of Miss Payne. I couldn't swear that she hadn't seen me and Kiffo, that she couldn't positively identify us, but somehow I doubted it. I felt convinced things had happened so quickly that she might have had her suspicions about the phantom sneezer and the target of Slasher's blood-lust, but that she couldn't be entirely sure. It gave me a curious tingle of anticipation to think she could be teaching me, thinking I was the prime suspect, but being unable to prove it. I wanted to be like one of those movie criminals who sneer derisively at the cops because they know that the evidence won't stand up in court. I wanted to say to her,

'Listen, bud, either you charge me or I'm out of here.' I wanted to see her frustration and hear her say, 'OK, Harrison, you're free to go, but don't leave town.'

It was a battle. On the one hand, I could barely walk. On the other, I was rigid with anticipation. I decided on a cold shower. For about ten minutes, I let the spray play over my injured foot, but it didn't do much good. It still looked like a diseased pig's stomach. After I dried myself off, I rummaged around in the bottom of my wardrobe until I found them. A pair of my dad's running shoes. They were unbelievably hideous – all piping and white canvas, the sort of thing that might have been in fashion in the mid-eighties but were now a testimony to bad taste. God knows why I had kept them. Perhaps, when I was younger, I had had fond ideas of clutching them to my chest in bed and sobbing over his desertion. I couldn't remember now. But they were the only items of footwear in the entire house that could cage the swollen bladder of my foot.

Even after swaddling my injured foot in a few layers of toilet paper, the outsize shoe was still incredibly painful. I couldn't even do up the shoelaces. In the end, it took me about twenty minutes to get dressed, with the Fridge shouting at annoyingly regular intervals for me to get out of bed and ready for school. Finally, I checked myself out in the mirror.

I cut a bizarre figure. Pretty standard from the ankles up, but I appeared to be wearing two large Persian cats on my feet. I looked like Minnie Mouse without the ears. I staggered down the stairs as if I had a length of curtain rod up my bum. The Fridge took one look at me and turned pale.

'My God, Calma,' she said. 'You look like Minnie Mouse. What on earth are you wearing those things for? And why are you standing like that?'

'They're fashionable, Mum,' I said, curling my lip in the manner of someone infuriated by parental ignorance. 'Everyone's wearing them.'

The Fridge nodded, still looking somewhat aghast. I knew I was safe with the old 'they're in fashion' trick. She had seen enough teenage styles to know that nothing, however bizarre and ridiculous, was out of the question. She chewed thoughtfully on a piece of toast and looked me up and down.

'Well, you look like you have a couple of snowdrifts on your feet. Still, if you're happy . . .'

I could finish the sentence for her: '. . . to look like a complete loser and fashion victim.'

I breakfasted on cornflakes, two Panadols and intermittent conversation. The Fridge kept trying to draw me out. She told me that I was looking like crap (thanks a lot), that I seemed depressed (and why wouldn't I?) and that I should talk to her about anything that might be bothering me (how? Through notes on her stained exterior?). Now I know I said earlier that I could really have done with talking things over with her, but to be honest the moment had passed. It seemed to me that a parent is there for emergencies – there's just no point in them arriving late, oozing empathy. The fire had burnt itself out and here she was, offering up a bucket of water to the charred remains.

Unfair? Is that what you're thinking? Yeah, well, you're probably right. But I guess I just wasn't in the mood.

Anyway, as luck would have it, the Fridge was leaving for work at the same time I had to take off for school, so she gave me a lift. I really hadn't been looking forward to the walk. In fact, just hobbling from the car to the canteen area, where I normally hung out between lessons, was enough to make me doubt the wisdom of going to school at all. Kiffo was there, smoking a cigarette. It always amazed me how he smoked in full view of the teachers on yard duty and nothing ever happened. Whenever a teacher looked in his direction they'd suffer from some sort of temporary blindness. Too much trouble to do anything about it, I guess. They'd have to write reports and stuff like that. Anyway, most of them smoked, too.

Kiffo took one look at my shoes and raised a quizzical eyebrow.

'Nice footwear, Calma,' he said. 'You look like . . .'

'Yes, thanks, Kiffo. I've been told already!'

We quickly talked over the events of the previous evening. It turned out that Slasher, for reasons best known to himself, had ignored Kiffo entirely and homed in on me. Maybe, with his superior canine faculties, he had come to the conclusion that taking a bite out of Kiffo's leg might constitute a serious health hazard. That *he'd* have to get a rabies shot. Whatever, Kiffo had seen very quickly that I was the target. He had spotted me leaping on to the fence and had taken a short cut to the other side, hoping to help in some way. I told him about the damage to my foot and the necessity of wearing shoes the size of kayaks. Like me, Kiffo didn't believe that the Pit Bull had got a good sight of us.

For the rest of the time before the bell we talked over the implications of what we had seen the previous night. For once Kiffo didn't have to convince me of anything. I mean you didn't have to be a genius to work out what was in that bag.

> *For one hundred and twenty-five thousand dollars. What was in the bag that the Ferret handed over to the Pit Bull?*
>
> **A.** *Bread-making flour.*
> **B.** *Sugar for a cake stall at the local school fete.*
> **C.** *The entire dandruff output of Melbourne residents in one calendar year.*
> **D.** *Pure heroin.*
> *Phone a friend? Ask the audience? Nah. Lock it in, Chris.*

We compared notes on the mystery man and agreed he had to be a drug lord. He looked like one of those characters who says, 'Well, Meester Bond, you have proved a worthy adversary but now I'm afraid that I will have to lower you headfirst into this tank of piranhas. Then, of course, I will find a reason to wander off aimlessly before your head touches the water, allowing you to perform a miraculous escape without spoiling your hairdo.' Hell, this guy looked as if he might have been thrown out of the Mafia for cruelty. In my admittedly fertile imagination I was already beginning to think that I had spotted a black patch over one eye and a thin, pale scar along his jawline.

In the end, though, no matter how much we thought we knew about the whole business with the Pit Bull, we didn't have any hard evidence and without that we'd be struggling to nail her.

'We should tap her phone,' Kiffo said.

'Genius, Kiffo,' I replied. 'And just how are we going to go about that?'

'I dunno,' he said. 'In the movies, guys just go up telephone poles. Maybe we could wire up her phone line to a phone we've got and then listen in.'

'The fact that you haven't a clue how to go about this doesn't dampen your spirits in any way?' I remembered all too well that in the last Science unit we had done Kiffo had scored four per cent. He'd answered the first question and then fallen asleep. Kiffo had always believed that letting teachers know what was in your head was akin to passing information to the enemy. 'Knowing your luck,' I continued, 'you'd pick the power line and barbecue yourself.'

'What about Tandy?' asked Kiffo, after a bit of back-of-the-head scratching. 'Maybe they'll have a kit.'

'A How-To-Tap-A-Phone Kit? Next to Build-Your-Own-Submachine-Gun and Devise-Your-Own-Thermonuclear-Device? Ah, yes. I think they've got them on special.'

'Yeah. All right, smart-arse.'

Kiffo screwed his face up further in concentration.

'Perhaps we could plant a bug on the dog.'

'Listen,' I replied. 'Firstly, I think Slasher has already got a full complement of bugs. Secondly, we haven't got a bug to put on him and thirdly, put a hand anywhere near that hound and you'd be minus at least three fingers. Get real, Kiffo. No, I think the only realistic option is to do what we've been doing already. Keep trailing her, wait for something else to happen. Something that we could go to the police with.'

By this time the bell had gone and we had wandered over to Registration. Miss Blakey, our teacher, was waiting at the door. She looked me up and down as I approached and then took me discreetly to one side. Kiffo sidled into the room.

'Are you all right, dear?'

'Fine, Miss. Why do you ask?'

'It's just that you are walking a little funny. Are you sure you're all right . . .' She looked around once or twice and lowered her voice conspiratorially, '. . . *down there*?'

'Certain, Miss. Down there has never been in better shape, thanks for asking.'

'Good. Well, anyway, Mr Di Matteo wants to see you in his office. Immediately.'

I could tell that this was going to be one of those days.

Let me give you a little bit of information about Mr Di Matteo, our respected Principal. I once asked Kiffo to break into the personnel files at the school and get the dirt on the Prinny. He turned up with the original letter of application:

Dear Sir,

I wish to apply for the position of Principal, as advertised in your Education Bulletin of 3 March. I am 50 years old and have looked this way since I was 20. For a period of three years, in my early teens, I possessed a rudimentary sense of humour though I have long since misplaced it. I do not like or understand children, who appear to me to be somewhat distasteful in their personal and social habits. I once had a creative thought, but have unfortunately forgotten what it was. Throughout my teaching career, I have relied on networking and unashamed arse-licking for the promotions I have received. In turn, I have promoted people like myself. As a consequence, every school I have taught at has been dominated in the upper echelons of management by grey and unimaginative minds.

I have continued to keep abreast of educational developments, recently completing my Advanced Diploma in Senior High School Information Technology. I am proud to be able to write Dip. Shit after my name. Given my background of mediocrity and managerial incompetence, I feel I am over-qualified for the position described. I also feel that your remuneration package of $120,000 per annum, plus company car, would allow me to comfortably see out my time to retirement.

Yours faithfully,

Liam J. Di Matteo

Actually, that's not true at all. I made it up. Sorry.

A summons to see Mr Di Matteo was a rare event. It could mean that something good had happened to you, like you had won a major competition and he wanted a picture of you with him so that he could send it out to the papers. Preferably a very large picture of him, with you peering in the background, like one of those people standing behind the reporter, trying to get their face on TV. Or it could mean you'd been caught doing something wrong. Seriously wrong. And the trouble was, I hadn't entered any competitions recently.

Sure enough, when I knocked on the door and was told to enter, I saw him sitting at his desk. The expression on his face was not the kind that inspires confidence. Not the kind that makes you think he is about to kiss you on both cheeks and say, 'My wonderful child, I am so proud of you!' Particularly since the Pit Bull was standing next to him. And, dangling from her outstretched right hand, she held a familiar and somewhat torn and battered red Converse shoe.

I felt a bit like Cinderella being confronted by Prince Charmless.

Chapter 12

The Prinny, the Pit Bull and pictionary

'Is this your shoe, Miss Harrison?'

I toyed with the idea of just giving my name, rank and serial number, but thought that this might make the situation worse. I decided to play for time.

'What shoe's that, Mr Di Matteo?'

'Don't be stupid, child. This shoe, the one that Miss Payne is holding up. Is it your shoe?'

'I don't think so, Mr Di Matteo. I normally buy mine in twos.'

Miss Payne slammed the shoe down on the edge of the Principal's desk, causing a flake of red canvas to flutter to the floor. If I had been hoping for the good cop, bad cop routine I was out of luck. This was going to be purely bad cop, bad cop. The Pit Bull glowered. (A good word, 'glowered'. A sort of a cross between 'gloomy' and 'lowered'.) Her features crowded in on each other, her shoulders tensed, and her eyes shot me a glance of pure hatred. Baleful. (Another good word.) Her face was positively overflowing with bale. You couldn't have fitted in another smidgeon of bale if your life depended on it.

'Don't get smart with me, Miss Harrison. You know perfectly well what the Principal is talking about. This shoe. Unless I am much mistaken, you often wear a pair of shoes identical to this. I also have reason to believe that you lost one of them last night. Now, what do you have to say for yourself?'

It seemed to me that she was right in one regard. Smart-arse comments were probably not going to help me out in this situation. I decided to play the helpful student, solving a minor mystery.

'May I look at it more closely? I do own a pair of shoes similar to this.'

Mr Di Matteo waved me forward graciously, as if he was the judge in a murder trial and I had requested permission to approach the bench. I picked up the shoe and pretended to examine it carefully. I nodded once or twice in what I hoped was an intelligent fashion.

'Ah yes, I can see the confusion,' I said. 'I do have a pair similar to this. Or should I say, I *did* have a pair. But mine weren't Converse. I wish, mind. Very expensive and good quality. You see this star, here?'

The Pit Bull and the Prinny both leaned forward. I was

starting to enjoy this. I felt like a forensic scientist pointing out fascinating and specialist facts on a murder weapon.

'This is a trademark of the Converse company. There are a number of other companies that, quite illegally, attempt to copy a popular brand, including the trademark. I have to confess that I did own a bootleg version of a pair of Converse shoes, but the star was nothing like this. As you can see, this star is neatly and tightly stitched.'

The Pit Bull and the Prinny both nodded. I think I had them hooked, like on the *Antiques Roadshow* – that TV programme where people bring in their antiques for expert evaluation. Pretty soon I was going to ask them how much they had paid for it and then tell them to insure it for two thousand dollars.

'The star on my inferior copy was very badly stitched. It might have fooled a non-expert at a distance, but close up it was an obvious fake. Another thing. The red on this shoe is of a very deep hue. That's quality dyeing. Mine was more of a dirty pink.'

I tossed the shoe back on to the desk.

'No. This is not my shoe, I'm afraid. Now, is there anything else I can help you with?'

Just for a moment I thought I was going to get away with it, that they were going to say, 'No, that's all. You've been very helpful.' Unfortunately not. The Principal leaned back in his chair and assumed his chief prosecutor expression.

'You say you have a pair like this. Would it be too much trouble for you to bring them in?'

I adopted a sorrowful expression.

'I'm afraid that's impossible. You see, I was watching a documentary recently. An exposé on bootlegging. I was shocked to discover that many companies employ child labour in undeveloped countries to make poor quality copies of well-known brands. These children are exploited disgracefully and I realised that by buying these fakes I was contributing to their exploitation. So I took them to Oxfam. The shoes, not the children.'

I could tell by the look on their faces that they knew I was lying through my teeth. To be honest, I was a touch annoyed. Did I look like the kind of person who wouldn't be moved by the story of child exploitation? I mean, what I had told them about the documentary was true. However, I couldn't really get too self-righteous since I *was* actually lying through my teeth about the rest. Miss Payne looked me up and down. I think the intention was to wither me with her contempt. However, when she reached my footwear her eyes nearly did one of those cartoon tricks where they come out on stalks.

'And these ... things ... are now your preferred footwear, are they?'

The three of us silently examined the monstrous white meringues on my feet.

'They might not be pretty, Miss Payne,' I said in a voice

dripping with sincerity, 'but they are the genuine article. I might look a little strange in them, but I am prepared to put up with that, so long as I know that no children have suffered in their manufacture. Besides, they belonged to my father. My father who left me when I was in Year 6. They . . .' I attempted a catch in my throat '. . . have sentimental value.'

What a bunch of garbage! I was starting to embarrass myself. But I could tell by the way the Prinny and the Pit Bull exchanged glances that they knew it was the end of the tenth round and they were way behind on points. Then I was worried that they'd ask me to take off my shoe and show them my foot. Not that it would have proved anything. I could have injured my foot in a thousand different ways other than having it used as a doggy chew. But after a moment of quiet reflection, I knew they couldn't really demand that I remove my footwear. It's one thing to search your bag, but quite another to demand that you expose parts of your anatomy to school authorities. Clearly, Mr Di Matteo had come to the same conclusion because he swept an exasperated hand through his thinning hair then waved at me to leave.

I turned and walked slowly towards the door. I had just touched the handle when Miss Payne spoke again.

'Just one minute, Miss Harrison. You seem to be walking in a very strange manner. If I didn't know better, I'd think that you had injured your foot in some way. Like being bitten by a dog, for example. Now I know that this couldn't possibly have happened to you, but I want you to listen carefully, Miss Harrison. If I ever find out that you have been following any member of staff, me for instance, then I promise you that this won't just be a school matter. I will prosecute with the full force of the law. Do you understand me, Miss Harrison? In theory, I mean?'

I tried a long-suffering glance of silent reproval.

'Of course, Miss Payne. As far as my walk is concerned, I realise that my gait is consistent with an injury. However, without wishing to be indelicate, it is an unfortunate side effect of a certain feminine problem. You know, *down there*.'

I loved the look on the Prinny's face as I turned to go. As I left the room I heard the Pit Bull say, 'You should see the nurse, Miss Harrison!'

Yeah, and you should see a plastic surgeon, I thought, as I closed the door behind me.

I filled Kiffo in at lunchtime. When I had finished, he turned to look at me, the flaming red hair standing up at bizarre angles, as always.

'All right,' he said. 'Time for you to take a back seat, Calma.'

'Forget it,' I replied. ' You don't get rid of me that easily. True, it's too dangerous for me to be lurking outside her place just at the moment. But she obviously didn't see you, Kiffo, or suspect that you were there last night. If she had, she'd have dragged you down to the Prinny's as well. I think you should carry on as normal. I'll give it a few days and then join you, when things have settled down. In the meantime, I'll try and check out the Ferret guy. Mind you, I've no idea where to start!'

Kiffo didn't even try to argue. He went back to kicking a footy about while I pondered the problem. I kept on thinking all through Science, which meant that I totally messed up the experiment and burned a large hole in a test tube with my Bunsen burner. The teacher had to spray my bench with that foam stuff, and evacuate the classroom. The whole class was extremely pleased with this little drama and for a while they forgot to be horrible to me. Until Sarah Parker said, 'She was probably dreaming about the Pit Bull! Love does that to you.' She clearly thought that she was an expert on that subject, since she had been going out with Clayton Rioli for about a month.

[Clayton Rioli – **Cancer.** You are a diseased little specimen with all the sex appeal of a bird-eating spider. This will prove no impediment to your love-life, however, since you are romantically involved with a primordial life form who cannot afford to discriminate in affairs of the heart.]

After that there was the usual chorus of jeers and immature comments, so I retreated back into myself.

The last lesson of the day – of the week – thank God, was

English. The Pit Bull thumped into the classroom and thirty bodies instinctively cringed in their seats. It reminded me of that Russian psychologist, Pavlov. He had this experiment with dogs. What he'd do is feed them when he rang a bell and after a while they would begin to drool whenever they heard a bell ringing, even if no food arrived. They associated the sounds with what they anticipated was coming next. Well, it was a bit like that with us. When the Pit Bull came into the room we knew what to expect.

This time, though, it was different. Instead of leaping straight for the jugular or ripping out entrails, she smiled. Well, I call it a smile, but it was more like a crack appearing in the centre of her face. It was unnerving.

'I would like to place it on record that you have all worked exceptionally well this week,' she said. 'There has been a remarkable improvement not just in your attitude, but in the quality of the work you have been producing. So today, I think we can afford a little relaxation as a reward for our efforts. What do you say to a game of literary Pictionary? I give you the name of a famous novel or poem and you draw pictures on the board as clues for the rest of the class who have to guess what it is.'

I knew what I wanted to say. Something to do with inserting the game into a place where the sun doesn't shine. I kept quiet, though. I knew what she was doing and I knew it wouldn't work. You can't terrorise students for weeks and then expect them to eat out of your hand or roll over on their backs to have their tummies rubbed. Just how stupid did she think we were?

'Yeah, Miss!'

'Great!'

'Can I go first?'

I looked around the class in bewilderment. What was going on here? Kids were smiling, putting their hands up in excitement. Melanie Simpson was rolling over on her back, exposing her belly. I felt betrayed.

'Why don't you begin the game, Kiffo?' continued the Pit Bull. 'I'll give you an easy book title, just to get us started. There'll be prizes for those who do the best drawings or get the answers quickest.'

Kiffo! She called him 'Kiffo'! No one other than his mates called him 'Kiffo'! He glanced at me across the room. It felt like the two of us were alone in a world that had just gone crazy.

'Nah, thanks, Miss,' he said. 'I'll sit this one out.'

'All right, Jaryd. That is your prerogative. So who'll start? Melanie, your illustration skills are excellent. I've got a title here that I think you will find challenging.'

And Melanie Simpson came to the front, looking like the cat who had not just got the cream, but had followed it up with a couple of succulent goldfish. What followed was fifty minutes of screaming laughter as twenty-eight kids had what looked like the best time of their lives. You got the impression that in fifty years they would be telling their grandchildren all about it. You know, sometimes human nature sickens me.

I felt like standing up and giving them all a lecture on basic psychology. When you've been savaged by a rabid dog, it might seem a welcome relief to have it licking your face, rather than trying to tear it off, but there's a limit to what the human mind can cope with. Violent extremes are unsettling, if not downright dangerous. They can lead to a nervous breakdown. Which was just what I felt like having as I looked around my English class. I would have preferred a normal lesson, with gnashing teeth and involuntary bowel movements. You knew where you stood with them. I was relieved when it was all over. There's only so much fun and happiness you can stand.

I went straight home after school and made myself a cheese and Vegemite toastie. The Fridge came home briefly, heated up some mess, and then was off to the bar where she worked five nights a week. She'd be home some time around midnight. I wanted to talk to her.

OK!! I know. I know what you're thinking. And I can't blame you for it. Moody bitch, that's me. Wants to talk one moment and then doesn't the next. I guess I was mixed up. But I'd got it into my head that I needed to discuss what was happening with another woman. The trouble was that the Fridge and I didn't seem able to talk any more. And I know it wasn't all her fault, but it sure as hell wasn't all mine either. She was fiercely proud after Dad took off. There was no way, for example, that she would claim any benefits for being on a low income, even though I knew for a fact that we were entitled. The one time I suggested it, she delivered such a lecture about spongers that I didn't have the courage to broach the matter again. The way I see it, earning your way was all well and good, but there were other important things in life as well. Like having a daughter who you had time to talk to, or a mother who was around a little bit. But I knew that I wasn't the one to tell her. And that made me lonely and sad.

I was half-hoping that Kiffo would turn up on his way to the Pit Bull stake-out, but he didn't. So I had a shower and bathed my injured foot. It seemed to be settling down. The swelling had subsided and the colours weren't quite so psychedelic. It was still a bit tender, but I could walk on it without looking like I had lost control of my extremities. Then I went to bed early and lay awake thinking over the events of the day, the cunning of the Pit Bull and the best way of tracking down a man you had only seen once, briefly, under a streetlight in the middle of the night. By the time I fell asleep, I was no nearer to a solution. As it turned out, I needn't have worried. I virtually fell over the guy the next day.

MAY: Primary school, Year 6.

You are sitting next to the red-haired boy in a quiet classroom. You are doing a maths test, working quickly because maths is easy for you. With fifteen minutes to go, you've finished and your eyes stray to the answer sheet of your neighbour. He is doodling a skull and crossbones. You notice that he has finished the first two questions, but the rest of the examination has not been attempted. You glance at the teacher who is sitting at his desk marking, his head down. Your hand gently slides his answer sheet towards you. You manage to get twelve of his questions answered before the time is up. It will be enough to pass.

You leave the classroom together. The boy touches you quickly on the shoulder.

'Thanks,' he says.

You look at him. Your expression is difficult to read.

'Fuck off,' you say, without malice.

Chapter 13

Working girl

I woke up late, about eleven. The Fridge was at work and the whole day stretched out before me. I decided to get a bus into the CBD. I'd stashed away twenty dollars of my pocket money and I fancied spending it on a blue halter-neck top I'd seen on a city market stall. Donning my pink and yellow glasses I headed off into the sunshine.

There's not much to do on a bus other than stare out the window or examine the graffiti on the seat-back in front of you. In this case, the only thing to read was 'Darryl is nuff' which was a little skimpy in terms of plot, though high on romance. Suddenly, out of the corner of my eye, I saw him. The thin little man. He was hurrying along a busy shopping street, looking like a man with a purpose. I caught a glimpse of his profile and then the bus swept me away. Without even thinking about it, I pressed the bell, praying that the next stop

wouldn't put me out of distance entirely.

When I got off the bus I was at least four hundred metres from the place I had spotted him. I walked back quickly, scanning the streets, but he had disappeared. It was really frustrating. Unless he had got into a car or hailed a taxi or something, he had to be around here somewhere. I decided to wander the streets and see if my luck was in.

For the longest time, it seemed it wasn't. Then, just as I was about to give up, I saw him again. I had stopped outside a restaurant and a familiar silhouette caught my eye. I peered through the window into the gloomy interior and there he was, sitting at a table with four other guys. They all looked like extras from *The Sopranos*. I glanced up at the sign above the restaurant. 'Giuseppe's'. That figured, I thought. They were probably planning to take out the Mayor with machine guns once they'd finished their pasta and meatballs.

So now what? I needed to hear what they were saying. I had this really strong feeling that if I could just get close enough, I'd get some crucial information. Two options presented themselves. One: I could go into the restaurant as a customer and sit at a table next to them. I still had my twenty dollars, after all. The trouble was, the lunchtime rush hour had just started and the restaurant was crowded. There was one small table in the corner that was vacant, but I'd have needed a boom microphone to listen in to their conversation. Second option: I could try lip-reading. I had done a lip-reading course in Year 8 – well, not really a course as such, more an introduction. Still, I had been quite good at it.

I moved a little further down the street so that I wasn't directly in front of the window. I didn't want the Godfather to look up from his garlic bread and find a large pair of lurid spectacles watching him above a mouth moving silently in translation. I crouched behind a parked car where I still had a good line of sight to their table. They say that nothing you have ever learned is entirely lost, it's just locked and filed away somewhere in your brain under 'completely useless information'. All I needed to do was find the key. I let my mind go blank and just watched the Ferret's lips moving, hoping the words would float unbidden into my consciousness.

And it worked! Suddenly I heard a little voice in my head saying, 'My bum was anointing the jelly and scotch.' Perhaps they were speaking in code. Maybe I'd got it slightly wrong. Perhaps it was really, 'My gun was pointing at his belly and crotch.' That would make sense, particularly if the person he was talking about had a very large, overhanging stomach. I concentrated again and this time picked up, 'If the telly welly bit the leopard hard my pants were wet with dew.'

It was no good. This was getting me nowhere. Anyway, my cover was blown when the driver of the car I was hiding behind accelerated into the traffic, leaving me crouched in the middle of the street and the subject of a few strange glances from passers-by. There had to be an option three, though I was buggered if I could think of it.

And then, like the first flash of lightning in a storm, the solution seared across my eyeballs. A blimp in a red and white checked uniform hove into view. It was Rachael Smith. She of the lesbian taunts. The one who had spread rumours about me to the entire English-speaking population of the world. She was a waiter at Giuseppe's! I watched as she leaned over a table with a carafe of water, smiling at the customers. They looked a little startled, but that might have been because she blocked out all available light. They also looked as if they were tourists. Rachael was probably going to tell them about me.

Now, I want some credit here. You will understand that of all people in the world, Rachael Smith is the one I definitely wouldn't wee on if she was on fire. Yet I needed her help. The fact that she was a loathsome putrescence wasn't going to deter me from talking to her.

I ducked down the side street beside the restaurant and found a back door which gave on to a storeroom. I stood unhappily among the vats of olive oil, looking for inspiration or Rachael Smith – whichever came first. I have to admit I was nervous. I have no idea if it is some sort of felony to be lurking with intent among industrial packages of lasagne, but I had sudden images of a police loudhailer crying, 'We know you're in there, Harrison. Come out slowly, with your hands on your head, kicking the tagliatelle in front of you.' Fortunately, at that moment another door opened and Rachael came in.

When she saw me, a huge, imbecilic smile spread across her plump cheeks.

'Calma Harrison,' she said, proving that she could remember a name overnight. 'Or should I say, *Gay*ma Harrison?'

'Great one, Rachael,' I replied. 'You must have been Oscar Wilde in a previous existence. Look, I'd love to exchange witticisms with you, but tempus is having a damn good fugit.'

'What?'

'Time flies. Oh, never mind. I have a proposition for you. I want to do your job for the next hour. No pay, of course. You keep that. I just want to do your work.'

She was immediately suspicious.

'Why would you want to do that?'

'It's personal, OK? I don't want to go into it. Just an hour. That's all.'

'What do I get out of it?'

'What do you mean, "What do I get out of it?" You get to sit on your fat ar— You get to relax, while I do all the work. No catches. Simple as that.'

'I dunno. I could get into trouble. Mind you, the boss is away today . . .' I could see the cogs whirring slowly. 'Have you waited on tables before? It's very skilled, you know.'

'Are you kidding? I was employee of the month at Pizza Pizzazz four times running. What I don't know about pizza and pasta isn't worth knowing.'

'I still dunno.'

'I'll give you twenty bucks.'

'Deal! But I want it up front.'

It was reassuring to know that Rachael's sense of obligation to her employers was so firm in the face of temptation. I handed over the twenty bucks and she handed over the uniform, a smocky number you could lose a sperm whale in.

'I'll be back in an hour,' she said, disappearing off through the outer door, probably in search of a cake shop.

As you may have guessed by now, I had absolutely no idea what I was supposed to do. However, the first step seemed simple enough. I put the uniform on. It was like a sail cloth. Doing a fair impersonation of a hot air balloon, I went out the door that Rachael had come in. Inside was a large anteroom and it was buzzing. Waiters were screaming around like dodgem cars. Chefs were yelling out orders, plates of steaming dishes were being slung on to a low aluminium counter where the waiting staff were collecting them. It looked like chaos. I didn't know where to begin. However, there was one woman who seemed a promising point of contact, on the simple grounds that she was screaming, 'Where the hell is that Rachael?'

I fronted up to her.

'Who the hell are you?' she enquired, without modifying the decibel count.

'Rachael had to go. An emergency at home. She'll be back in an hour. I said I would cover for her.'

The woman looked me up and down and she didn't seem pleased with what she saw.

'Hell, hell, hell. I do not need this. I really do not need this.'

I explained that I was an ideal replacement, but she was only half-listening. Occasionally she would yell at some poor waiter. 'Not the lasagne for *table 4*, you complete idiot. *Table 6*. And where's the wine for *table 9*? What the hell have I done to deserve this?' Finally, she turned her attention to me.

'I haven't got time to argue. You're on tables 3, 5 and 7. There's a carbonara ready for 5, two side orders of salad and a fettuccine special. Table 7 are just about to order. Take the wine list. Table 3 will need the dessert menu in about ten minutes. Come on. Get moving. Hell!'

And she was off, presumably to lash a few of the scurrying minions with a bull whip. I moved to the counter and collected what looked like a carbonara and a fettuccine special. Listen, I might exist largely on a diet of microwaveable chicken offal and frozen pizza, but I watch all the cooking shows on TV! All I needed to do now was find table 7. Or was it table 5? I breezed through the swing doors into the restaurant and looked around. My Mafia man was still sitting with his cronies, but it was obvious that my order was not for them. I decided the best bet was to spot two people who weren't eating, but looked hungry.

It didn't take long to find them, I can tell you. I hurried over with a look of abject apology.

'The fettuccine and the carbonara? I'm so sorry to have kept you waiting. Still, I can promise you that it'll be worth the wait.'

I plonked the plates down in front of them and was about to rush off when the man stopped me.

'Excuse me! I ordered the carbonara and my wife ordered the fettuccine!' He pointed down at the plate in front of him. It took me a while to realise what he meant. I had the plates in the wrong places. My first reaction was to tell the lazy bastard to switch them himself. I mean, how much effort does it require to swap plates? Instead, I apologised and switched things around. I was halfway back to the kitchen when I heard his voice again.

'Excuse me!'

I felt like I was attached to him with a piece of elastic. I hurried back.

'Yes?'

'Side salad?'

'Where?'

'We ordered side salads.'

'Ah, yes, I believe you did. Would you like them now?'

'Well, it would be nice to have our salad with the main course, rather than with dessert!' Part of me wanted to warn him not to get into a battle of sarcasm with me. If there were a sarcasm Olympics, I'd be first choice to represent my country. However, I gave a simpering smile and scurried off.

'Excuse me!'

Now I had excused him twice already, and my patience was starting to fray. I came back wearing one of those smiles that looks as if it has been ironed on.

'The carbonara is cold.'

'Would you like it hot?'

The man's face turned red. Under other circumstances it would have been an interesting phenomenon, but I quickly grabbed the plate and shot back to the kitchen. I had to get a replacement dish, pick up two side salads, take an order from someone somewhere in the room (pick the customers who were starting to eat the tablecloth?), find a bottle of wine, open it, give it to whoever ordered it and then take a dessert order from someone somewhere else. I decided that I could afford a small detour.

I approached the Mafia table and hung around, hoping to pick up a little of the conversation. After a minute or two, the Ferret turned to look at me.

'Can I help you?' he asked. I was disappointed to notice that his accent, far from being Sicilian, was dinky-di Oz. Still, that didn't mean a whole lot. In most of the gangster movies I had seen, they all had American accents. I couldn't really expect him to have half a goat draped around his neck and a shotgun slung on his back. I went for a winning smile.

'Are you enjoying your meal, sir?'

'It's very good. Thank you.'

I smiled again, but he seemed to expect me to leave.

'Can I get you anything, sir?'

'Nothing at all, except a little privacy. That would be nice.'

'Of course, sir.'

I didn't really have much choice. Plus, I still had a job to do. I went back into the kitchen and found the microwave. It was a huge, industrial-sized thing with enough dials and knobs to confuse an airline pilot. I shoved the plate in and put it on high for a minute. Then, in the recesses of Rachael's uniform, I found a pad and a pencil and went off to take the order from table 7. Or table 5. It wasn't difficult to find them. They were the four drumming their fingers on the table and looking around with a desperate air. I rushed up and apologised.

'Never mind, never mind,' said a middle-aged guy. 'Just take the orders, please.' His tone was acerbic.

'We want one linguine al troppo with extra parmesan and the spinach pesto; one calamari Mediterranean with a green salad on the side, NOT on the plate, that's with Thousand Island dressing, naturally; one alla Borghese WITHOUT the parmesan but WITH the mange tout; and a Fabrizio ravioli, provided it's al dente. Plus, we'll have four Campari de Sodas.'

I nodded furiously and wrote down 'four pepperoni pizzas'. I recognised him, you see. Mr Gray, my Maths teacher in Year 8. Frankly, I thought that screwing up his order was completely inadequate payback for a year of differential equations and a classroom management style that consisted entirely of purple-faced invective, but you have to take your chances when you can. Plus, with any luck, I'd be out of there before smelly things started to hit the fan.

'And where's the wine list?'

'On its way, sir.'

I ran back to the kitchen, slapped the order on to the table and grabbed the carbonara from the microwave. Plate was bloody hot. I did the little 'ouch, ouch' bit as I ran back, getting the thing down on to the tablecloth moments before my fingers started smoking. Now, what was it next? Ah, yes, the dessert menu for someone or other. Boy, this was a tough job. My fingers were smarting and my forehead was developing a thin sheen of sweat that I confidently expected to drip on to someone's plate. I hadn't moved three paces before I was stopped in my tracks by an agonised scream behind me.

The man with the carbonara had gone an interesting shade of purple and was pointing desperately at his open mouth. Thin wisps of smoke were issuing from the gaping orifice. I scuttled back.

'Remarkable taste, isn't it, sir? I trust it's to your satisfaction.'

For a moment, it looked like he was going to collapse on to the table. I hoped to hell I wasn't going to have to do the Heimlich manoeuvre. That was tucked away in my brain next to the lip-reading skills. Luckily, he recovered a little and, gasping like a gaffed fish, finally found his voice.

'Are you mad?' he spluttered. 'This thing is boiling! It's approaching the surface temperature of the sun! It's cauterised my lips!'

No pleasing some people, I thought. First it's too cold, now it's too hot. I was about to point this out to him in my normal tactful fashion when the supervisor shot out of the swing doors like a greased torpedo and was at the table in slightly less than half a second.

'Is everything OK, sir?' she asked. Clearly a born optimist since it was apparent to everyone that the answer was unlikely to be, 'Never been better, thanks for asking.'

'No, it bloody well isn't. First the food was stone cold and now it's like molten lead. I have never, in my life . . .'

The supervisor gestured for me to go. I was happy to oblige, I can tell you. To be honest, I had my suspicions that I'd blown my tip from table 7. Or was it table 5? Still, it gave me an opportunity to check out the Mafia table again. I swept past the foursome with the mad mathematician and he took the opportunity to pluck at my sleeve.

'Wine list?'

'No thanks, sir. I'm trying to give up.'

And then, just when I thought the whole thing was destined to remain a complete and utter disaster, a monumental waste of time, I had the biggest stroke of luck . . .

Scene 141, take 1

Interior: *Italian restaurant. Medium shot. Don Carlo Vermicelli is sitting at a table. He has a napkin tucked into his shirt and there is a plate of pasta and meatballs in front of him. To his left is his consigliore, Michael Cornetto, wearing a sharp suit. On his right is a thick-set man with dewlaps and interesting acne. This is Luigi 'Powertool' Scarlatti, a man whose expertise with chainsaws, drills and orbital sanders does not extend to the production of rustic outdoor furniture. Behind the group two men stand, silent, with goats slung across their shoulders and pump-action shotguns strapped to their backs. Cut to close-up of Don Carlo, who appears to have padding inside his cheeks. Or it might be a couple of errant meatballs.*

Don Carlo: He'sa not showing me respect. I needa respect. My family needsa respect. And I tell you, Michael, that I respect his family, but he don't respect my family. There'sa no respect. So I wanna his family whacked. With respect. Then maybe he respect me, respectfully, like I respectfully respect him. Whaddya want, kid?

Medium shot. Calma, disguised as a waiter. In one fluid movement she flings off her huge smock uniform, exposing a charcoal grey suit and Uzi submachine gun. The group is stunned into immobility.

Calma: The game's up, Carlo. We have it all on tape. Yes, that's right – the goats were carrying wires. You're going down, Carlo. Down for a long time. We've got you cold on supplying narcotics, running the East Side numbers racket, prostitution, extortion, loan-sharking, tax evasion, laundering detergent and riding a bicycle on public roads without a helmet. It's a federal rap and you're all out of options. You'd better come quietly.

Cut to close-up of Don Carlo.

Don Carlo: Who are you, kid?

Calma: Harrison. FBI Special Agent Calma Harrison. But my friends call me . . . FBI Special Agent Calma Harrison.

Cut to close-up of Michael Cornetto. His eye twitches. Cut to Luigi Scarlatti. His hand reaches inside his jacket and grips the handle of an electric paintgun. Cut to Calma. Her eyes narrow. Slow motion. Luigi pulls out the paintgun. Calma squeezes the trigger of the Uzi and bits of goat, meatball and exterior emulsion spray all over the walls . . .

CUT!

Scene 141, take 2

Interior: Italian restaurant. A top-heavy female waiter in a uniform tailored for an African elephant scuttles towards a table of four businessmen. She hovers on the fringe, in the forlorn hope that she might appear inconspicuous. She overhears a snippet of conversation.

The Ferret: . . . we mustn't miss this opportunity, gentlemen. There is a huge shortage of top-grade heroin on the streets at the moment . . .

The waiter drops a carafe of water on to her toe, screams and dashes through the suddenly stilled room and out the swing doors.

CUT! That's a wrap!

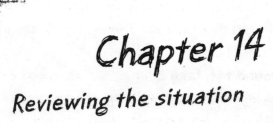

Chapter 14

Reviewing the situation

Have you ever seen that old movie *Singin' in the Rain*? It's pretty sad, generally, but there is this great scene where Gene Kelly dances down the street. It's pouring with rain, but he is really happy, splashing into puddles and singing and dancing his socks off. I felt just like that. As soon as I got out of that restaurant, I felt exactly like old Gene Kelly must have done. OK, it wasn't pouring with rain, I didn't have an umbrella and I wasn't singing or dancing, but other than that it was a pretty faithful re-enactment of the whole scene. I even did a little skip around a lamppost. You know, hanging on with one hand and swinging all the way round. I couldn't wait to tell Kiffo. I was so happy.

Until I collided with a large woman who'd been walking a pace or two in front of me. I suppose my momentum, as I completed the lamppost circuit, must have thrust my feet into her back. It was careless of me, but I had felt so full of energy that I couldn't contain myself. Her shopping bags went flying. There were apples and cans of stuff rolling all over the place. The woman fell to her knees. I felt really awful.

'Oh God! Sorry,' I said as I bent down to help her to her feet.

She turned around and I found myself face-to-face with the Pit Bull.

'Miss Payne!' I said. 'I am so very sorry! Please forgive me.'

I tried explaining. I told her that it was a pure accident, that I had no idea whatsoever that she was walking along that street, that I had been feeling particularly excitable and had simply acted on impulse. I even tried explaining about *Singin' in the Rain* but I think, by that time, I had lost my audience. I was scurrying around picking up cans of tuna, dusting off apples, wiping grit and traces of doggy doo off her bananas and I suppose I might have seemed just a touch hysterical. Meanwhile, she stood there like an ancient monolith, Uluru or something. Still babbling, I pressed the rather sorry and mis-shapen groceries into her arms.

'So there you go, Miss Payne. No harm done, eh? Just a freak accident. Thousand-to-one chance really! Well, I've taken up enough of your time. I'm sure you've got better things to do than spend your Saturday morning talking to . . .'

'I don't know what I have done to deserve this,' said the Pit Bull. Her voice was very quiet and there was a catch in it, like she was on the point of crying. Her lip even trembled. 'You have followed me to my home, you have harassed and badgered me. And now, you assault me . . .'

'I didn't mean to,' I said. 'It was an accident. I swear I . . .'

It was as if I hadn't spoken.

'. . . in broad daylight, you assault me. I'm sorry, Calma, but I've had enough. I can't take it any more.'

And she turned and limped along the street. I fought the impulse to run after her and try explaining again. I knew there was nothing I could do and that talking further would probably only make the situation worse. Boy, she seemed upset! If I hadn't known that she was up to her wrestler's armpits in illegal stuff, I'd have felt sorry for her. I really would. There was even a part of me that admired her performance. The trembling lip, the catch in the voice. If I didn't know better, I'd have taken it for genuine emotion. What an actor!

OK, I was worried. I admit it. Frankly, the last thing you need when chasing a drug dealer is a drug dealer who knows you are chasing her. I had visions of me ending up in concrete boots at the bottom of a river or forming part of the foundations for the new shopping centre. Nevertheless, I was also feeling pretty proud of what I had achieved in the restaurant. Digging in my purse I found a dollar. Enough for the bus ride to Kiffo's place.

When he opened the door, he looked like he had been through the hot wash and fast spin cycle.

'God, Kiffo,' I said. 'You look as if you've been ridden hard and put away wet. What on earth have you been doing?'

'Staking out the Pit Bull's place. All night, if you want to know the truth.'

No wonder he looked exhausted. He could hardly stop yawning long enough to invite me in. I had one foot over the threshold before I remembered what his place was like. So I suggested that we go for a walk. Anyway, it looked like the only thing that would keep him awake.

As we walked, I asked him how the stake-out had gone.

'Nah, nothin' doing. I got there about ten-thirty and she was definitely in. I could see her through the kitchen curtains. When I left, about six this morning, she hadn't budged.'

He was absolutely exhausted. His whole body was slumped, as if he were carrying an intolerable burden. I slipped my arm around his shoulders. I could feel his muscles tighten instinctively, but he didn't shrug me off.

'Wait till you hear my news!' I said. 'I've been busy, too.'

And I filled him in on my undercover work at Giuseppe's and my run-in with the Pit Bull later. When I told him what I had heard the Ferret saying, he brightened up considerably. It was as if the news washed away his tiredness. His eyes sparkled with excitement.

'I told you, Calma. I told you there was something going on. Now we know.' *He* was almost dancing down the street now, bandy legs skipping from side to side.

'Hang on, Kiffo,' I said. 'We *suspect* that there is something going on. But suspicion is a long way from knowing. Listen, if this were a TV show, there'd be some balding guy in a shiny suit, saying to us, "Harrison and Kiffing, I need more than circumstantial evidence. Sure, we could put out an APB, bring her in, but her attorneys would make damn sure that the case would never stand up in court. She'd walk. Get me solid proof I can take to the DA. It's our only chance of an indictment." You see what I'm getting at?'

'No.'

I grabbed Kiffo by the arm and sat him down on a park bench that was grubby even by his standards. Scrambling around in my bag, I came up with a battered envelope and a rather leaky red biro.

'Let's jot this down, shall we?' I scrawled three columns on the back of the envelope.

Behaviour	Suspicions	evidence
Pit Bull gets a phone call in the middle of the night.	She's arranging a deal with criminal underworld.	None — hearsay from burglar.
Pit Bull has suspicious meetings in the middle of night.	As above.	The word of two schoolkids.
Ferret gives Pit Bull a bag with white stuff in it.	Heroin/coke drop.	None.
Ferret talks about heroin drought.	Business meeting, discussing possibilities for organised crime.	None. Hearsay. Could be an innocent conversation among concerned citizens about state of society.

I handed the envelope to Kiffo.

'You see? There's nothing here. Nothing that we could use if we went to the police. They'd laugh at us. We need hard evidence, Kiffo. Something that isn't just our word against two respected members of society. Fingerprints, tape-recordings, photographs. That kind of thing.'

I was starting to reconsider my career aspirations. Maybe I should become a police officer. Chief Superintendent Calma Harrison, the scourge of the underworld. Tough, streetwise, folding twenty dollar bills into the top pockets of grasses, busting bent coppers, feared and respected. 'She's tough, but she's all woman!' Or maybe a lawyer! I could just see myself pacing up and down in front of a jury, hypnotising them with my impeccable logic and oratory skills in an emotional closing address.

> So I put it to you, ladies and gentlemen of the jury, that all the facts point in one direction and one direction only. The defendant, Miss Payne, or as she is known in the seedy drug underworld, the Pit Bull, has for years been polluting the streets of our city with the most evil of substances – heroin. She has been preying upon the young and the helpless for the saddest and most despicable reasons of all – personal gain. Did she care that our nation's youth were dying in the streets? Did she care about their

untold misery? She did not, ladies and gentlemen of
the jury. She did not. I ask that we send a message
in this case. A message to the law-abiding citizens of
this wonderful country of ours. A message to the
parents of those who have died and are continuing
to die. A message that we care, that we are deter-
mined to root out this cancer in our society. I call
upon you to hand out the most severe sentence the
law will allow. I know that I can rely upon you all
to do your duty. I rest my case.

I'd almost forgotten that Kiffo was still there. He folded the envelope and handed it back. We started to walk again.

'I guess you're right,' he said finally. 'But if it's hard evidence we need, then hard evidence is what we'll get. If I have to stake out her house every night, we'll get it!'

'Maybe so, but after what she said to me today, you'll have to get it by yourself. I can't go near her house again. I mean, I'll do what I can, but I can't risk getting into trouble with the police. That's what she threatened me with in the Prinny's office. Prosecution. And then it'll be game over.'

Kiffo snorted.

'You don't have a clue, do you, Calma?'

'What do you mean?'

'Prosecution, trouble with the police, all that stuff. You've no idea. Like I've got no idea with a poem, you've got no idea about the law. There ain't many things I'm an expert on, but the police is one. Let me give you a lesson. Firstly, police time. They're so busy tracking down thieves, doing drug busts and handing out speeding fines that they've got no time to scratch their arses, let alone chase a schoolkid for hanging around a teacher. Secondly, you haven't done nothin' to her. What's she gonna say? There's this kid who talked to me outside my house, then my dog chewed her shoe while I was meeting someone in the middle of the night. No, officer, I didn't see her, but she had a pair of red shoes. And she bumped into me in town, on a busy street. They'd laugh at her, Calma. Maybe, if we were real lucky, charge her with wasting police time. And thirdly, she's up to no good herself. So who's the last people she's going to contact? The police, that's who. Nah, you don't have to worry about the Pit Bull. She's not going to do nothin'. '

Kiffo fell silent. Given that he had probably used up an entire month of vocabulary in one hit, I wasn't surprised. He reminded me of one of those geysers in North America: dormant for years, maybe the occasional dribble, and then – boom – you find yourself drenched.

I don't think either of us had planned it, but we had wandered, by degrees, into my neighbourhood. I thought about what Kiffo had said and he did have a point. If we had no evidence against the Pit Bull and the Ferret, then what evidence did they have against us? And given the soaring crime rates in the city, why would the police be bothered with something so trivial? It seemed much more likely that the Pit Bull was trying to frighten me with threats she knew she would never be able to follow up. Scare me a bit and hope that would be enough to discourage me.

So I probably would have been much encouraged by Kiffo's analysis if it hadn't been for a couple of things. I could see the driveway of my house, and my mother's car was there. She should have been at work. But that wasn't the most worrying thing. By far the most worrying thing was the police car parked behind our old Ford.

Kiffo scratched behind one ear.

'Course, I could be wrong,' he said.

AUGUST: Primary school, Year 6.

It is the end of the school day. You leave the
classroom with the red-haired boy. The sun is
shining and there are a couple of hours of daylight left. You feel good. You have put to the
back of your mind what is waiting for you at
home. It is not something you want to think
about: the darkness, the confined rage and your
parents' faces closed to each other.

As you pass through the gates of the school,
the red-haired boy turns from you and runs
towards two young men leaning against the school
fence. You watch. One young man is about seven-
teen. He has red hair and eyes that look through
you, as if he is focusing on something just
beyond your vision. The other young man is
muscled. He has a shaved head and tattoos on his
arms and neck. He says nothing.

Your friend throws himself into the arms of
the red-haired young man. He looks up into his
face and you see something in his expression that
you have not seen before. It looks like love. The
older boy ruffles the hair of the smaller boy and
then his gaze turns towards you. You are alarmed
by his stare.

'Who's your girlfriend, then?' the older boy
says.

Chapter 15
The lull

I walked very slowly towards my house. Kiffo said something, but I don't know what it was. All I know is that by the time I got to my front door he had gone. I'd heard of tunnel vision before – that medical complaint where you can't see anything at the borders of your vision – but this was my first experience of anything like it. It was as if everything else had disappeared. I could see the old off-white door, with its familiar scratches and stains. And it seemed as if it was approaching me, looming larger and larger while I stood still. Nothing existed beyond it. If a truck had been coming down the street I wouldn't have heard it, wouldn't have seen it. The way I was feeling deep inside my numbness, I'd have been happy for it to hit me. Anything to keep me away from that door.

I saw my hand reach out and push against the panel, just above the ragged wound where I had crashed my bike when I was eight years old. The paintwork felt cold. A hinge complained feebly and briefly as the door swung open. It had obviously been left slightly ajar. The dark hallway stretched out in front of me. Little specks of dust swirled in a thin beam of light that angled in from outside. At the end of the hallway, the kitchen door was half-open, though I could see nothing except a corner of the fridge. Low voices drew me slowly towards them. Towards the kitchen door, the corner of the fridge and whatever lay to one side of it.

I could have run. Even then I could have run. Waited until the police had gone. Until my mother had gone to work again, or gone to sleep. Put it all off to another time. Prepared my defence, settled my mind. Maybe I should have run. But I know now that nothing could have stopped my slow progress towards that door, that confrontation. I was powerless to resist it.

I pushed open the kitchen door and, with that one small movement, stopped the voices instantly. I went inside. At the kitchen table, facing me, was my mother. She looked up at me as if meeting a stranger. I could see wetness on her cheeks, but her eyes were dry. One hand fidgeted with an unlit cigarette. The other plucked nervously at a loose strand of hair. It was as if a powerful hand reached inside me then and squeezed. It hurt so much that I gasped.

Sitting opposite Mum, his back to me, was a police officer. He had turned in the chair and was looking at me over his left shoulder. For a moment, I had the strangest notion that he was someone I knew, someone who had dressed up as a police officer. You know, as if he was going to a fancy dress ball. And then I knew why he was familiar. It was Constable Ryan, the school-based police officer. I had seen him hundreds of times at school. He'd often wave to me and smile, exchange the occasional, 'G'day.' He wasn't smiling now. To his right, standing up, was a female police officer. She didn't seem much older than me. Her face was slightly twisted, as if something had slid from the plane of her face and then halted. It gave her a fractured look that wasn't entirely unpleasant. There was the hint of a light in her eye, like a smile that she couldn't release. It was strange. A strange expression in that company. In that kitchen.

Everybody looked at me for a while and then I sat in the chair to Constable Ryan's left. I placed my elbows on the table and linked my fingers. What I wanted to do was keep my eyes firmly on my interlocked knuckles. I knew that would be bad. But I couldn't look at Mum. So I forced myself to look at the female police officer. I tried to fix my eyes on the point of her chin. But what took my attention most was the handle of her gun. I didn't like it. I didn't want it in my kitchen. And I couldn't escape the certainty that I had brought it here. The silence gathered. I could hear the tiny electronic click of the kitchen clock.

And then the talking started. I can't remember everything

that was said. I don't want to remember everything that was said. But I remember enough. And the thing I remember most vividly is not the words themselves, but rather the absence of words. Throughout the whole time, Mum did not say a thing. Not until the police had gone. I hated that most of all. I don't think she made a sound. I don't think she even moved. It was if she had been frozen there or was simply a part of the furniture. Like the fridge.

In the end, what Constable Ryan said wasn't of much importance. I don't mean that the way it sounds. Because he said serious stuff. It's just that it was the *situation* that was really important, the fact that he was there in my kitchen at all. The words were accessories after the fact – though each one cut into me like tiny slivers of glass. He told me about the laws governing stalkers. He told me that what I was doing was illegal. Even if we ignored the fact that I was breaking the law, he said, there was still the pain and suffering that results from a person's privacy being invaded, the sense that they can't go anywhere and feel safe. He told me about terror. That it was emotional brutality, an act of violence as real and as undeniable as physical violence. But we couldn't ignore the fact that I had broken the law. He told me about trespass orders, juvenile courts, criminal records. Even if I wasn't prosecuted, and he couldn't promise that I wouldn't be, I was still guilty. This was not a game, he said. This was not a schoolgirl prank. I mustn't fool myself into thinking that all I had done was make a nuisance of myself. This was serious.

All the time he talked, I kept my eyes fixed firmly on the chin of the woman opposite. I said nothing as Constable Ryan continued. He told me that I had previously been of good character. The school had reported that I had never been in any trouble before. A search of the police database had revealed nothing. All the reports indicated that I was an intelligent student and, before this, a responsible student. I had great things ahead of me. But whether I achieved those things was up to me. I had important decisions to make. And one of those decisions would have to be about the people I chose to associate with. He told me that he had known many good kids get into trouble because they got in with the wrong crowd. We all knew that he was talking about Kiffo, though his name was never mentioned. He told me also to think about the pain I had caused my mother, who was doing her best to raise me properly, who was working hard to make sure that I had the best start in life. Did she deserve to be called out of work to hear all this about her daughter? I remember thinking vaguely that they must have got her work number from the school's records. I wondered how they had broken the news to her.

And then they went. I remained seated. I couldn't swear to it, but I think the woman gave me a small smile before she drifted out of my field of vision. But it might have been a facial tic. I can't be sure. Mum saw them out. I heard the front door close and her slow footsteps returning to the kitchen. She sat down in the same chair. I still had my eyes fixed on the point where the woman's chin had been. Now there was a pepper grinder on a shelf, occupying the line of sight she had vacated.

Inside me, something was breaking. It was like when you have to throw up. It comes from the core of your being. But I was throwing up feelings, chunks of feelings that burned my throat. And my mother still stayed silent. I was scared.

Chapter 16

The storm

Mum didn't exactly break the silence. She shattered it, smashed it to pieces, destroyed it. One minute, we were sitting there, a still life of misery, the next, she erupted.

Ask me now what I should have done and the answer is easy. I should have kept quiet. I should have taken it. Mum had a right to be angry, she needed to lash out. And maybe I needed to take some punishment too. I've tried since to look at it from her point of view. I've tried to imagine what it might be like if I had a daughter and the police came to my workplace. No warning, no hints. I know that I would react as she did. Probably worse, knowing my tendency to be verbally trigger-happy, to use words that fire and tear.

So I'm not proud of my part in the argument. But, as you must know by now, I can't help myself sometimes. When there's a word brawl around I'm always going to find myself in the thick of it. Mind you, I wasn't in top form.

'What the hell is going on, Calma? What is going through your head? A stalker? My daughter, a stalker? Following a teacher around, attacking her . . .'

'I didn't attack her!'

'Hanging around her house at night. Why, Calma? Tell me! Because at the moment I don't know what is going on.'

'I didn't attack her!'

'That's not what the police say. They say you could be charged with assault or stalking or both. Charged, Calma. Court. Magistrates. Juvenile detention. And I see that you don't deny you were following that poor woman! Kept that quiet, didn't you? So why should I believe you didn't attack her as well? Why should I believe anything you say?'

'Well don't believe me, then. I told you I didn't attack her. It was a stupid accident, that's all. But if you think I'm a liar, fine.'

'Answer my question, then. Why? Why have you been doing all this?'

'Like you'd be interested!'

That was a mistake. A big mistake. I see that now, but it just came out, like these comments always seem to do, without my permission. Mum smashed her arms down on the table. I jumped. I had never seen her so angry or so hurt and betrayed. I knew the storm was building but I was helpless to do anything other than be swept along by it.

'How dare you?' she screamed. 'How dare you say that to me? For years I've been bringing you up by myself, working myself into the ground so I could give you the best of everything. Nothing I have done, in all that time, has not been for you. Do you think I like the work I do? Do you think it's a great job standing at a check-out all day, scanning bloody packets of pasta for bugger-all money? And when I finish there, I come home, get something to eat and then spend hours at the pub, pulling beers, putting up with drunken bastards making lewd comments. Do you think I like that?'

'I never asked you to do any of it!'

'No. You didn't have to. I did it of my own free will. I did it for you. So that you could have a good education, have all the things you need to make a success of your life. Because there's one thing that terrifies me, Calma, and that's the thought of my daughter working in a supermarket or a pub for the rest of her life, scraping by, never able to dig herself out of the poverty trap. So don't tell me I'm not interested. I don't deserve it.'

And she didn't. I know that. I knew it then. But it's hard, when you're under attack not just from your own mother but also from your own conscience, to do anything except fight back with all the dirty tricks you can find. I needed to build up some indignation, a sense that I was being unjustly accused, so I could bury the knowledge that I was in the wrong.

'You're not doing it for me, though, are you?' I yelled.

'You're really doing it for yourself. So you can say to me, "I've got a shit life and it's all your fault!" You don't need to do two jobs and you know it. We are entitled to benefits, Mum, but your pride won't let you claim them.'

'I will not take money from the government, Calma. I will not. I was brought up to work for my money. I will not be a sponger and neither will you!'

'How many times, Mum? How many times do we have to have this conversation? It's not sponging. It's what we're entitled to. It's what you pay taxes for . . .'

Mum grabbed the sides of her head in both hands as if trying to physically stop the words from entering. But I wasn't going to let that happen.

'And if you stopped being such a bloody martyr for a while you might be able to spend some time with me. You know, do what mothers and daughters are supposed to do. Have a relationship, talk, that kind of thing.'

That got through. Mum brought her hands down. Tears of pain, or rage, made her eyes glisten. Her fingers curled into hard knots.

'So it's all my fault, is it? Is that what you're saying? That if I spent more time with you, you wouldn't be getting into trouble with the police?'

'Well, there's a bit of truth in it, isn't there? Other people that I know have parents who talk to them, care for them, look out for them. They have parents who are there. I don't have anyone. I hardly ever see you. How do you suppose that makes me feel? I've got a mother but I forget sometimes what she looks like. And, OK, I don't go without stuff. But even you, Mum, even you must know that's not enough. Give me less stuff and more time.'

Mum got up and stomped around the kitchen.

'You're too bloody smart for your own good, Calma Harrison. You think it's that easy? You don't even know how much the rent is on this place. You don't know what a bill looks like. You have your air con on all night, but you never think how much money it costs. Look around. Do you see plenty of things? New microwave? A dishwasher? Hell, no. Do you know the last time I went out? Do you know the last time I bought myself some clothes? Well, neither do I! And it's not because I'm stashing the money away somewhere. We spend what I earn just keeping a roof over our heads and food on the table. So don't lecture me about finances, 'cause you know nothing about it. God, do you think I wouldn't spend more time with you if I could? Is that really what you think? And I'll tell you another thing. You're not going to blame me for this. I'm not taking responsibility for your behaviour, do you hear?'

I jumped up out of my chair. I wasn't going to let her have the advantage of the moral *and* physical high ground. And anyway, if I didn't start moving, physically, the emotional energy would be hard to sustain. We faced each other, like boxers, both bloody and battered but unable to stop swinging.

'No, Mum. Don't take responsibility. Why break the habit of a lifetime? Just keep earning the money. But don't think that entitles you to the right to ask me what's happening in my life. Because that's the one thing you haven't even tried to earn!'

I thought she was going to hit me then. I even flinched in anticipation. But she kept her hands at her sides, though I could see the effort it took. Her voice, when she spoke again, was cracking at the edges, splintering under a weight of emotion.

'So I haven't earned the right to an explanation? I don't deserve to be told why the police came to my workplace to tell me that my daughter is behaving in a criminal fashion? I don't deserve to know?'

'No. I don't think you do!'

'Well, what about this Kiffing boy? The police said you had been – what was the word? – "associating" with an undesirable character, a young man known to them as a criminal. He's got a police record! Did you know that?'

'I don't care, Mum! I don't give a crap about any of that.' I was suddenly aware that I was shouting at the top of my voice. 'Kiffo's a friend. He's been there for me when I've needed him.'

'Are you sleeping with him?'

I leaned close in.

'Mind your own damn business! That's the kind of thing that a daughter might talk about to a mother. And until you start behaving like a mother, I'm telling you nothing.'

She hit me then. A sharp crack across the side of the face that twisted my head around. The storm had broken. There was a silence. My cheek felt numb and then it tingled with the onset of pain. I turned back to face her. Her expression was wide, frightened, as if she couldn't believe what had happened. I could see that she was saturated with sorrow. It was oozing from every pore. Her hand crept upwards towards her mouth in contrition. But I was hardened. I had my grievance now and nothing was going to take it away from me.

'Calma . . .'

'Go to work, Mum,' I said quietly. 'Just go to work, will you? There's nothing else to be said here.'

And I walked out of the house. As I opened the front door, I could hear great gulps of grief coming from the kitchen. The sound of her tears as I left was like a song of victory. I felt washed of guilt.

You watch the three young men and feel as if you are intruding. Part of you wants to walk away because you are embarrassed, but another part wants to stay. You have never seen your friend look so happy and you are curious.

'She's not my girlfriend,' says the red-haired boy. 'She's just a friend.'

'Let's get a photo,' says his brother. It has to be his brother. The resemblance is too marked.

'Like the camera?' says the man with the tattoos. 'Our latest acquisition. Japanese job.'

He takes photos of the two red-haired boys and then you and your friend are persuaded to stand up against the school railings. You feel shy as the shutter is clicked. But you also feel good.

'It's important to keep a record,' says the older red-haired boy. 'Memories are sometimes all you have.'

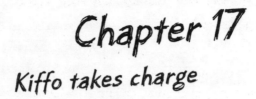

Chapter 17

Kiffo takes charge

I want you to think well of me. Whoever you are. But I also know that it's pretty unlikely you will be feeling very charitable towards me right now. I don't blame you. I acted very badly. I know that. But you need to understand a couple of things. The first thing is that I didn't have to tell you everything. I could have toned it down, made myself look more reasonable than I was, and you would never have known the difference. So now you know. I can be a real cow. But at least I'm an honest cow. The second thing is that I think some allowance should be made for the stress I was under at the time. I was terrified. I can't even begin to describe how I felt when I saw that police car outside my house.

[Constable Ryan – **Capricorn.** You will find that your reputation as an easygoing, paternal figure is severely jeopardised as a consequence of scaring the crap out of impressionable and possibly misguided young women wearing glasses.]

Have you ever been in an argument where you've just got more and more unreasonable and unfair and cruel, simply because you're angry and frightened? If you have, then you'll understand about that crazy urge to hurt the very person you know you've wronged. I don't know why. All I know is that I felt it strongly. I think, in Mum's situation, it would have been sensible to have left the whole business alone for a while, given me time to chew on things before leaping in with recriminations. At least, that would have been the best theoretical option, the textbook approach. I also know that it's an option I wouldn't have taken. Too volatile, that's me.

Anyway, I left the house ablaze with indignation – me, that is, not the house. Mind you, given the heat generated by the argument, it wouldn't have been surprising if smoke *had* been pouring from the roof. There was only one place to go. Only one place I wanted to go. After what Mum had said, I had to see Kiffo, if only to punish Mum further. Besides, where else could I go? As far as friends were concerned, I wasn't exactly bursting with options.

I wasn't even aware of the journey. The adrenalin rush was still going strong and I knew it would take time to subside. I covered the ground like a thing possessed, probably pushing old ladies out of my way for all I knew. Before I had time to think I was outside Kiffo's house, storming up the path towards the front door. I had my hand raised to knock when I heard it. The sound of voices raised in anger told me I wasn't the only one having difficulties with a parent.

Now. Imagine this is a survey in one of those teen mags.

You have just turned up at your best friend's house and hear a fierce and personal row going on between your friend and his or her parent. Do you:

a) *leave quickly and never mention it again because you are worried about embarrassing your friend;*

b) *walk away, but remain close in case your friend needs to talk to you;*

c) *intervene and attempt to act as a mediator between the two parties;*

d) *put a glass against the door and listen, with your tongue poking out of the corner of your mouth?*

You go for b), right? Gets you ten points and ultimately a character description along the lines of, 'You are a true and trusted friend with the emotional maturity of a forty-three-year-old marriage counsellor.' You'd go for b), but you'd actually do d). Am I right? All right. Just as long as you don't get judgemental on me.

Actually, I didn't need a glass. A soundproof booth would not have cut out the grisly details. This is what I heard.

[*Parental Advisory Warning: The following scene contains strong language and medium-level violence but, thankfully, nothing in the way of nudity. It is not recommended for audiences under the age of fifteen.*]

Kiffing Senior: You're a ****ing lazy ****, that's what you are. A pile of ****. Get the **** out of this ****ing house.

Kiffing Junior: **** off, you ****** ****. Call me ****ing lazy! That's ****ing rich, that is, you ****, you ****** old **** bunch of ****.

Kiffing Senior: Just like your ****ing brother! A useless piece of ****. Go on, ****ing **** off, you *****.

Kiffing Junior: Don't you ever, ever mention him to me again, or I'll ******** kill you, you ******!

Kiffing Senior: **** you and your ****** brother! ***** and ***** the *****, ****** and ****** with ****all the *****, ****** ****ing ****!!

Inanimate object: Smash!

The door burst open and a familiar hunched figure swept past me as if I didn't exist. Within seconds, another figure appeared at the door. He yelled a farewell to his son that, roughly translated, meant, 'I no longer consider you the favoured fruit of my loins and your reappearance in this household is not something that I am anticipating with any great enthusiasm.' Kiffo halted briefly to answer with something along the lines of, 'I no longer respect you as a paternal caregiver.' Roughly translated, you understand.

Standing there, I came to the slow realisation that I was unlikely to be invited in for tea, muffins and a chat about the weather. This was confirmed by Mr Kiffing looking me up and down and then requesting that I leave the immediate environment. A believer in economy of language, he communicated this in only two words. I took his advice.

[**Mr Kiffing** – **Aquarius.** Family troubles are in evidence today and complications may ensue. You will find that your customary excellent communication skills are compromised by prodigious blood alcohol levels. Still, **** it.]

Catching up with Kiffo took some doing, but finally, puffing hard, I got into step. He didn't take any notice of me but kept muttering under his breath. From the little I could decipher it was clear that he wasn't thinking about what to buy for Father's Day.

'Kiffo!' I said. 'Hang on a moment. I can't keep up with you!'

Only then did he stop and turn to look at me. It was as if he hadn't any idea that I was there at all.

'Calma,' he said, his voice fragile around the edges. 'Where did you come from?'

'Never mind,' I said. 'Let's just sit and get our breath back.'

We had arrived at a small park. I say 'park' but it wasn't really anything so grand. Just a square of sparse, wilting grass, with a couple of sad, rusted swings in a corner. I doubt if any kids played there, but judging by the state of the ground the local dogs had adopted it as their communal loo. We wandered over to a concrete bench and sat down.

I decided to say nothing about the mild disagreement between father and son. That's part of the problem with Kiffo. Some things are conversationally out of bounds and it doesn't matter what you do, you're never going to break through the barrier he puts up. I don't know – I still don't know – how I could feel so close to Kiffo, so intimate in a way, yet be excluded from so many important parts of his life and his past. Sometimes, I guess, you just have to ride with it. You know, accept people for what they are, because if you push it too far, you drive them off. And then you really are alone.

(That was a statement written by Calma Harrison, authorised by the Federal Committee of Staggeringly Unoriginal Homilies on Human Relationships, Canberra.)

We sat for a while, stewing in our own worlds. I knew there was precious little chance of Kiffo initiating a conversation, so I started. I told him about the interview with the police and the argument with Mum afterwards. He scratched his head thoughtfully. It was like he was glad to have a change of mental environment.

'You're not taking all that seriously, are you?' he said.

'Well, I thought I might, Kiffo. You know, when the police come along to your house and threaten to lock you up for committing a crime, then – call me old-fashioned if you like – I thought I might take it just a bit seriously!'

'Nah. They're bluffing.'

'I don't care, Kiffo. I don't give a stuff! If they're bluffing, then they've succeeded. I throw in my hand. Game over.'

'So you're out, is that it? You're not going to try to get the Pit Bull?'

'I thought that was what you wanted!'

'It was.' Kiffo ran a hand through his hair. 'It was. But . . . it's like you said, Calma. We're in this together now. We've come too far.' He looked uncomfortable, his eyes flicking everywhere but never making contact with mine. 'I . . . I need your help.'

I nearly fell off the bench. For Kiffo to say something like that he must have been desperate. It was like him confessing to buying Nikki Webster CDs. I glanced over. He was sitting forward, his hands nervously interlocked. If ever there was going to be a time, this was it.

'If you're serious, Kiffo, then you've got to stop lying to me,' I said.

'What do you mean?'

'You and the Pit Bull,' I said. 'What is there between you? What happened in the past? Tell me that and I'll believe that we are truly together on this.'

That shook him.

'I . . . I don't want to talk about it, Calma,' he said.

'Then you're on your own.' I meant it, too. I couldn't keep on with this, not with half-truths and half-stories. So much for my resolution not to push! I waited. After a time Kiffo sighed.

'All right,' he said. 'Yeah, I'd seen the Pit Bull before she turned up at school. Years ago, in Primary School. My . . .' He shook his head. 'I saw her with . . . family, you know . . . before all that stuff happened. We went to her house, just the two of us. Twice, maybe three times. I sat by myself, while she and him . . . I dunno what they did but I didn't like her then and I don't like her now. I didn't trust her. That's it. That's all.' He looked at me and there was agony in his expression. 'I don't want to talk about it any more, Calma.'

I put my arm around his shoulder. You might not think it,

but that was more information than I had been expecting. For Kiffo, it was like baring his soul. And it made sense to me, knowing what I did. I could see more clearly what was driving him on.

'OK, Kiffo,' I said, gently. 'Count me in. What are we going to do?'

Kiffo sighed and leaned forward on the bench, head down. There was a long silence while he contemplated a dried-up dog turd between his shoes. Finally, he leaned back with the air of a man who has come to a momentous decision.

'Right,' he said. 'You can't go near the Pit Bull. And I can't stake out her place by myself. Not every night. So, it's time to call in a professional. It's time to pay a visit to Jonno.'

Chapter 18

Jonno

It is not often that the discerning buyer can find a property of this potential at this price. The well-established gardens boast some unique decorative features, including a burnt-out Holden and an amusing assemblage of ancient motorcycle skeletons and their rusted constituent parts. A delightful counterpoint to this rococo landscaping is the rockery, imaginatively comprising empty beer bottles and pizza cartons. For those who might feel that art is intruding too much on nature, there is also a palm tree that, with a little TLC, might not yet prove to be terminally diseased.

And the landscaped gardens are just the beginning! Right from the moment you push over the gate and prop it up against the wall, you cannot help but be impressed by the domicile itself. All expense has been spared to make this a quality home. The front door is just one of the surprises in store. Rather than hanging it at right angles to the doorframe in the conventional fashion, the enterprising owner has cast it at a jaunty angle, thereby allowing any available breeze to naturally air-condition the living space! And isn't it often the case that homes exclude the outside world rather than embracing it? Well, in keeping with the traditional architectural designs of Bali, this home's living space is a continuation of the great outdoors, with gaping holes in the flyscreens, walls and roof ensuring tropical living at its finest!

I gaped at what was, presumably, the place where Jonno lived. There were buildings in Baghdad that had received multiple doses of laser-guided missiles and were in better shape. Kiffo and I walked up to the door, kicking aside empty beer bottles. I grabbed him by the arm.

'Who is this guy, Kiffo?'

'Someone, all right?' he said, not altogether helpfully. 'Someone we need. Just let me do the talking, Calma. Jonno can be a bit funny with people he don't know.'

I had a bad feeling about this. Something told me that Jonno was not going to be the kind of guy you'd want to have a conversation with about the current state of Australian ballet or the latest contenders for the Booker Prize. This impression was confirmed when Jonno finally came to the door after Kiffo's repeated hammerings.

The first thing I noticed was the vest. It was torn and badly stained, as if Jonno had a problem finding his mouth with the soup spoon. But the shape of the vest attracted more attention. It was all lumpy and disfigured, like someone had poured eighty kilos of builder's rubble into it. Jonno, clearly, was a body builder. He had all those revolting veins that stand out on the biceps like relief maps of river systems. His muscles caused him to stand with his arms splayed. He looked over-inflated.

Not content with muscles of alarming proportions, Jonno had decorated them with a bewildering variety of tattoos. A snake curled up his left arm and disappeared behind his neck. A dragon breathed fire up his right. In the few spaces left by these creatures there was a series of vicious portraits of native Australian fauna, none known for being cute or cuddly. No koala to be seen, unless it was a bit of fluff disappearing down the jaws of a great white shark.

It was difficult to tear my gaze away from his body, but I felt that it was probably wise to do so. Jonno didn't seem the kind of guy you could stare at without inviting trouble. I let my eyes wander up to his face and then wished I hadn't. He had one of those long bush beards you could hide a wallaby in. The facial hair might have been some attempt to compensate for the lack of hair on his head. His dome glistened in the sunlight. It was a curious effect, as if his head had been put on upside down.

The thing was, I had seen Jonno somewhere before! God, you're not likely to forget something that looked like that in a hurry (*Crimestoppers? The Children's Illustrated Book of Psychopaths?*). But I couldn't place him. I decided to let my unconscious mind work on the problem for a while and smiled in my most engaging fashion. I couldn't help thinking that at any moment he was liable to rip my arm off and beat me to death with the soggy end.

[**Jonno – Taurus**. Your sensitive and aesthetic nature is much in evidence today. You will find opportunities to engage in fruitful and creative activities, like the gratuitous bludgeoning of old people or tearing the heads off chooks with your teeth.]

Fortunately, I never found out if this was his intention because Kiffo broke the threatening silence.

'Wassup, Jonno, you ugly bastard!' he said.

This did not strike me immediately as the safest opening conversational gambit with someone who was clearly an axe-murderer, or at least in serious training for it. However, it soon became clear that I was unaware of the correct social protocol in this situation because Jonno appeared to take no offence. Instead he smiled, revealing two chipped front teeth and an awful lot of blackness surrounding them.

'Wassup, Kiffo, you arsehole!' he replied.

I wondered if I was expected to join in the general exchange of insults but decided to keep quiet, as Kiffo had instructed.

'Need a word, mate,' Kiffo said.

'No worries,' Jonno replied. 'Come in.'

Look, if it's all the same to you, I'd sooner skip the description of the inside of Jonno's house. To be honest, I've blotted most of it out, the way some people do when they've been victims of a particularly unpleasant and traumatic experience. All I want to say is that the outside of the place looked warm and comforting in comparison. Still, to be fair, Jonno was a perfect host. No sooner were we inside the door than he pressed a couple of bottles of beer into our hands and got himself another. It took all my strength to unscrew the bottle top. Jonno ripped his off with his teeth, providing an obvious explanation for the deficiencies of his dental work. Now, I can't stand beer but I couldn't take the risk of spurning Jonno's hospitality. So I nursed mine carefully as I perched on the edge of a sagging sofa, trying to keep the minimum of buttock in contact with the minimum of material.

Kiffo, as he had promised, did the talking.

'Now, Jonno. Me and Calma here want some information about a woman, the Pit Bull. She's a teacher at our school. She's giving us trouble. We need to know who she meets in the middle of the night and what they talk about. We think she might be a dealer.'

Jonno frowned.

'A dealer? Be news to me. I know all of 'em in this area. Always possible, I s'pose. Someone new in the territory. So that's it, is it? A straight tail job?'

'Yup. As much information as you can get, soon as possible.'

'And the address of this pain?'

Kiffo gave it to him, but he didn't write it down or anything. Maybe that was a skill he had yet to acquire. He just nodded.

'And what's the rate?'

'You tell me, Jonno.'

'Well, I dunno. Let me think.'

This should be interesting, I thought. A bit like watching a dog ride a bike. You're not surprised it's doing the job badly, you're just surprised it can do it at all. The silence stretched.

'I'll want one of those new DVD players,' he said finally. 'You know the kind – remote control. Japanese job.'

'Right,' said Kiffo.

'And a good selection of DVDs. Let's call it twenty. And

none of that romantic comedy crap. Thrillers or horror.'

'Right,' said Kiffo.

'Plus a decent stereo system. Ni-cam. Surround sound. Japanese job.'

'Right,' said Kiffo.

'And a carton – no, make it two, of beer.'

Japanese job? I thought to myself.

'Right,' said Kiffo. 'The beer you can have up front. I'll drop it round tomorrow. The rest when you get the information.'

'Oh yeah?' said Jonno. 'And how do I know you'll come up with the goods, eh? What's my guarantee?'

'Well,' said Kiffo, 'I know if I double-cross you, you'll come after me with a baseball bat. And you've got more muscles in your big toe than I've got in my whole body. And you'd never give up 'til you'd found me, even if I ran to Tasmania.'

'Yeah,' said Jonno. 'You've got a point, mate. I'll take the job. Get me beer by tomorrow. I'll get in touch when I've got some news. All right?'

'Done,' said Kiffo. 'Right. We'd best be off, then. I'll see you tomorrow, you ugly bastard.'

'Yeah, catch ya later, arsehole.'

Kiffo flipped his empty bottle of beer through the window, where it exploded on what must have been a small mountain of broken glass. Jonno belched loudly and did the same. Give me credit here! If I had been in some Mongolian outback settlement and everyone was eating sheep's eyeballs or camel's testicles or something, I would have joined in. Follow the rules of the culture you're in, that's my motto. So I tried. Unfortunately, my beer bottle was still full to the brim, so I sent a small fountain across the room, drenching the sofa and what passed for the carpet.

This might have passed unnoticed. After all, the place was so disgusting that nothing I could do would lower the standard. But my aim wasn't great either. I missed the window by two metres and smashed a small standard lamp in the corner of the room. Jonno and Kiffo glanced at the damage.

'And a lamp,' said Jonno.

'Right,' said Kiffo.

It was only when we were two hundred metres away from Jonno's place that I allowed myself to relax. It felt like all my muscles had gone into involuntary spasm. I also realised that the whole time we had been there, I hadn't said a single word. It's not often you can say that about Calma Harrison! Kiffo, however, was walking along without a care in the world, rollie clamped between his lips, red hair bobbing above a dense smoke cloud.

'Kiffo,' I said. 'Where the hell did you dig him up from?'

'Jonno? He's all right,' said Kiffo nonchalantly.

'All right? "All right" for what? Neanderthal man? God, you've got some strange friends, Kiffo.'

Kiffo spun on me.

'He's not a friend! If you must know, I hate the bastard. But he's a pro. He'll get the job done. No worries.'

I should have shut up, but that's always a problem with me.

'Well, what was that about getting him stuff? DVD player, stereo. How are you going to manage it?'

Kiffo pulled on the last of his cigarette and flicked the butt into someone's yard.

'Yeah, looks like I'm goin' to be doin' a bit of shopping the next couple of days,' he said.

'Using what for cash?'

Kiffo looked at me as if I'd lost my senses.

'Haven't you heard, Calma? Cash is in the past.' He flexed his fingers. 'I prefer the interest-free, long-term loan option. Very long term.'

We parted company not long after that – me to wander around aimlessly until I felt it was safe to go back home, Kiffo to start his shopping spree, I guess. I didn't like to ask any more questions. I didn't want to know. It was getting dark when I turned into my street. My intention had been to check out the place. If Mum was home I was going to wander around for a while. Luckily, her car wasn't there and the house was in darkness. I let myself in, stuck some frozen lasagne in the microwave and then took it up to my room. At least my bedroom had a lock on it. I wasn't going to get into any more conversations with Mum. I was still mad at her. Or at least it suited me to be mad at her. I needed the excuse for non-communication.

As I lay in bed that night, I felt more lonely than I had done in my entire life. I thought about the day's events. It had certainly been busy – the Ferret, Giuseppe's, the Pit Bull, the police visit, the argument with Mum, and Jonno. No one could say that life was dull. But for all that, I felt desperate. I could take no consolation in the idea that we were making progress in the Pit Bull mystery. The threat from the police kept spinning in my head. I was a criminal. And even if I put that down to a mistake or to exaggeration, I certainly couldn't pretend I didn't associate with criminals. My relationship with my mother hadn't exactly been ideal before, but now it seemed to be torn beyond repair.

And overlaid on all that was the knowledge that I was without a real friend, other than Kiffo. Don't get me wrong. I'm not ashamed of him or anything. Far from it. But, as I've said before, there are just some things you can't talk to Kiffo about. Some things I'm not allowed to visit. Not properly. And sometimes, just sometimes, you need a conversational map where the boundaries are open and there's no legends saying, 'Here be dragons!'

Let's be honest. My life was a mess.

Chapter 19
The promise

[Calma Harrison – **Virgo.** Sensitive, kind, intelligent, given to occasional forays into the criminal underworld.]

Doubtless if I had read my stars they would have said something like: 'Your life is a mess and you feel that things can't get any worse. Do not worry. By Monday, you will have found that they can.'

I spent Sunday in my room, except for those times when Mum left the house to do the shopping or whatever. Then I'd rush down the stairs, stock up on anything I could find in the fridge and watch some telly. As soon as I heard the car on the gravel outside I'd take off up the stairs again and lock myself in my bedroom. Once or twice Mum came up and knocked on the door but I ignored her. Childish, I know, but it seemed like the easiest option. I really wanted her to go to work, but she must have had the day off, or just rung in sick or something.

Naturally, I spent a fair amount of time contemplating my situation. There could be no doubt that I was up to my neck in the brown, smelly stuff. But then I remembered that my grandmother used to say of some people that they could 'fall down the toilet and come up smelling of roses'. Maybe it wasn't all over yet. Maybe Calma Harrison could yet emerge from the excrement with an aroma of patchouli. It all depended on what happened with the Pit Bull, obviously. If we could expose her, then I could just imagine the reaction.

Children, I expect you are wondering why I have called an emergency Assembly today. Some of you might also be wondering why Miss Payne has been led from the hall in manacles, escorted by four SAS men in camouflage gear. I feel you should know that Miss Payne has been masquerading as an English teacher, something that will not come as a surprise to those of you who were in her classes. But none of us suspected she was also using her position here to distribute hard drugs to students, the school janitor and certain members of senior management. I said none of us suspected, but that is not strictly true. I call upon Calma Harrison and Jaryd Kiffing to step forward to receive the highest honours the school can bestow. For these students, with no help from any authorities – indeed despite the barriers erected by people like myself, who should have known better – these fine, upstanding students have exposed her for the heartless, cold monster she is. On behalf of the entire school, I offer my full and sincere apologies to Calma and Jaryd, in addition to my formal resignation from the role of Principal, a job that I am clearly unfit to hold. The Police Commissioner here will now present these two students with the Distinguished Medal of Honour, a cheque for ten thousand dollars and a certificate proclaiming them joint winners of the Young Australian of the Year award, prior to us chairing them around the school grounds to the tune of Advance Australia Fair. Let's hear it for Calma and Jaryd.

Yes. A lot was riding on what Jonno could dig up. That was one of the reasons I decided I had to go to school on Monday morning. I sure as hell didn't feel like it. In fact, throughout most of Sunday, the thought of going made me feel physically sick. But on Monday morning I waited until Mum had left for work and then shot down the stairs, grabbed a quick breakfast and rushed off. It wasn't just the hope of Jonno turning up trumps either. I had had a brilliant idea and I needed to run it by Kiffo.

Now, do you want the ever so slightly good news, the bad news, the other bad news, the yes there's more bad news or the completely, holy crap this is disastrous, news? OK.

The bad news: I got a note in Home Group to go to see Mrs Mills.

The ever so slightly good news: I had been taken out of the Pit Bull's English class.

More bad news: there was no other class to go into, so I would have to spend my English lessons in a little room by the Assistant Principal's office that was normally reserved for the kind of student who couldn't be trusted in classrooms. We had plenty of them at the school, the kid who couldn't go five minutes without uttering an obscenity or who felt duty-bound to dismantle the walls or the person sitting next to him.

Yet more bad news: I had to listen to Mrs Mills for about six hours as she went on about how she would be there to support me, while really she was trying to get me to dish up the dirt. I blocked all of her deliveries with a straight, dead bat. Appropriate, really, since a straight, dead bat was exactly how I thought of her.

And can there really be more bad news: the Pit Bull's classes were, according to Kiffo's reports later in the week, being received as the most enjoyable activity since the invention of masturbation. The last act of a desperate woman, according to Kiffo, but I didn't care if it was the first act of

Henry the Eighth. I knew what she was up to and it wasn't going to wash with me.

The most catastrophic bad news: well, you'll have to wait for that. First, let me tell you about the idea I wanted to run past Kiffo. We found each other at recess. It wasn't difficult. All you had to do was look for the two students who were the biggest Nigels in the entire place and you'd have spotted us. We sat down on one of those concrete benches on the edge of the oval.

'Kiffo,' I said. 'I've had a brilliant idea!'

'Oh, yeah?'

'I'm going to write it all down.'

'What?'

'Everything. The whole business with the Pit Bull. Everything we've seen, heard and done.'

'That's what you call a brilliant idea, is it?'

'Yeah. Seriously. Listen, we've talked about getting proof, but so far we've got nothing to show the police. I mean, yeah, I hope Jonno will come up with something solid, but it would still be a good idea to have a record of all that's happened up to now. You know, in case we forget anything. Something that'll show the police that we're not just a couple of kids making up stories, but serious investigators making a serious report. Come on, how could it hurt?'

Kiffo thought for a while.

'Still not what I'd call a brilliant idea, but I suppose it

might be worth it.' His eyes brightened. 'We could stick it in a safety deposit box, with instructions to our lawyers to open it in the event of our suspicious deaths. I saw a film once where they did that.'

I wasn't going to point out we didn't have a lawyer or a safety deposit box or any prospect of getting either.

'Exactly, Kiffo,' I said. 'Like insurance.'

'Right. Go for it,' he said. 'But, Calma, you've got to promise me one thing.'

'Sure.'

'I don't want you bringing ... him ... into all of this. You know what I mean. I know you, Calma, but what's gone on in the past isn't important. And I don't want his name mentioned. Do you hear me?'

'But Kiffo . . .'

'No, Calma. I won't listen. Not to that. If you're going to write about all of this, then I don't want him a part of it. Not a mention of his name. I need you to promise.'

I thought for a while. He was wrong. I knew that. But I also knew that there was going to be no way I'd be able to convince him of it. Anyway, I guess he had a right to make it a condition.

'All right, Kiffo,' I said finally. 'I promise.'

Chapter 20

Answers

'You shitheads!' he said. 'You shitheads are the biggest dick-heads I've ever met.'

You might remember that I never got round to telling you the worst piece of news – the 'just when you thought things couldn't get any worse, then something comes and kicks you up the arse' piece of news. It happened on Thursday after school. Jonno was waiting for us, leaning up against the school railing, smoking. I noticed, without surprise, a can of beer in his hand. Kiffo and I stopped outside the gates and Jonno looked us up and down, taking a final gulp of his beer before crushing the can in his hand and tossing it away.

'You shitheads!' he said. 'You shitheads are the biggest dick-heads I've ever met.'

'Whaddya mean?' said Kiffo.

Jonno just chuckled and shook his head.

'What a pair of dickheads!' he repeated.

'Look,' I snapped. 'Just tell us, will you? I don't want to stand around out here listening to insults, particularly those that are inconsistent about the precise composition of our heads. I don't remember that being included in the price. And, frankly, I've been insulted by better people than you. Certainly more articulate . . .'

Jonno put his hand close to my face and pointed. The glowing end of a cigarette wavered millimetres from my eyes.

'You watch your mouth, lady,' he said. 'Where I come from, we don't make no difference between punching a woman or a bloke. So if you want to keep those specs on the outside of your face you'd better shut up.'

I decided to shut up. Jonno didn't look the sort of person to make idle threats.

'Yeah, all right,' said Kiffo. 'Let's stick to business. Because if you start on my friend here, we're goin' to find ourselves fallin' out. Big time. I might be half your size, but you know me, Jonno. If I get it into my head to fight you, you'll have to kill me before I'll stop.'

Jonno looked at Kiffo, as if weighing things up. Then a big grin spread across his face.

'Never short of balls, Kiffo. I'll give you that. Right. I've done the job, but you aint gonna like the results. Subject's name is Payne, aged 45. She *is* into drugs. But she's not push-ing. She's a volunteer for DARP, the Drug and Alcohol

Rehabilitation Program. They have a 24-hour hotline. Payne goes out on calls maybe two, three times a week, to deal with junkies and alkies. Tries to keep them straight. She's not a drug dealer, for chrissake. She's a pillar of the community. Probably get a medal.'

Jonno flicked his cigarette butt away and produced a can of beer from a side pocket. Did he have a cool-box in there? Kiffo and I looked at each other. I could see denial written all over his face. As for me, I knew. I knew, with that awful sense of inevitability, that what Jonno had said was the truth. I could almost taste the bitterness of it.

'What about that bloke Ferret-face?' said Kiffo, an air of desperation in his voice.

Jonno popped the ring-pull and took a big swallow.

'Name is Collins, a director of DARP. Doctor, apparently. Big shot.'

> *Giuseppe's. A group of businessmen. 'We mustn't miss this opportunity, gentlemen. There is a huge shortage of top-grade heroin on the streets at the moment ... and we must hope it stays that way, if we are to rid our society of this appalling disease.'*

'Nah!' said Kiffo. 'It can't be.'

'I'm telling you straight,' said Jonno. 'Two nights I followed her. One time she met Collins at this hall place. That's how I got to check him out as well. Anyway, this hall. It's a sort of safe haven, a place where junkies go to get decent needles, hot food, that kind of stuff. It's what she does, Kiffo. I seen it with me own eyes.'

Calma and Kiffo stand on a pile of milk crates as they watch Miss Payne and Dr Collins talking inside the Drug Rehabilitation Centre.

Jonno prised himself away from the fence.

'Look,' he said. 'Got to go. Business appointment. I'll expect payment by this time tomorrow night, Kiffo. Come round to my place. I'd hate to have to come round to yours. Know what I mean?'

If Kiffo heard, he gave no sign. He was still shaking his head as Jonno strolled away down the road.

'You're wrong, Jonno. You're wrong,' he said. But his voice was almost a whisper. I reached towards him and linked arms. It was some indication of his state of mind that he didn't resist, didn't even seem to notice.

'Come on, Kiffo,' I said. 'I'll buy you a coke or something.'

He turned towards me.

'You don't believe it, do you Calma? You didn't buy any of it.'

'Yeah, Kiffo,' I said. 'I bought the lot.'

'Why?'

'Because it fits. Because it's what happens in real life, not the stuff we've been spinning. Don't you see? This whole thing, this whole fantastic adventure. We wanted to believe it. It was brilliant to think that a teacher we hated was also a criminal. But we were wrong. It's not good enough just to *want* something to be true. Because then we're simply part of a game – a terrific game, an exciting game. But in the end, only a game. And now we know, Kiffo. We know. It's game over.'

Kiffo plodded on for a few more paces, his eyes fixed on the ground. But then he stopped, grabbed me by my free arm and swung me round to face him.

'Not for me, Calma,' he said. 'Not for me.'

I shook my head.

'Come on, Calma. Think,' said Kiffo. 'How do we know Jonno is telling us the truth?'

'Why would he lie?'

'Why? 'Cos it's second nature to him. He can't do nothin' else. What if she bought him off? What if she realised we were on to her and she decided to cut Jonno in? What if he's working for her? What if he always has been?'

'If, if, if. If your aunt had testicles, Kiffo, she'd be your uncle! It doesn't make sense.'

'What about that bag? The one with the white stuff, that the Pit Bull took from the Ferret?'

'I've no idea, Kiffo. Maybe it was medication. It might

have been instant mashed potato for the junkies' dinner for all we know!'

I put my arm around his shoulders and he didn't remove it.

'I know you've put a lot into this,' I said. 'We both have. And it's difficult sometimes to accept that all the hard work, all the emotional and physical energy, has been for nothing. That we've wasted our time. But we've got to accept it. Give it up, Kiffo. Cut our losses. It's time to get back to normal.'

Kiffo's face twisted in concentration. He could never win a rational argument with me and he knew it.

'OK, Calma,' he said, finally. 'Just one more try. Give me that. Just one more go. If we don't get nowhere, then I give up. Come on. It's not much to ask, is it? A last chance?'

Maybe I was feeling a little confused and dispirited by the events of the week, but I felt myself weakening. He was looking so intently into my eyes. Pleading almost.

'I'm not going anywhere near the Pit Bull, Kiffo. No way.'

'You don't have to, Calma!' Kiffo was so excited by the implied agreement of my last statement that he was almost shaking. 'You don't have to. We go after what's-his-name, Collins, the Ferret bloke. One day. One day, Calma. We get nothing, that's it. Finished!'

'One day? Daylight? No messing around at night?'

'Swear! It gets dark, we're done.'

'When?'

'Saturday.'

I pretended to consider it. In fact, I knew immediately that I couldn't refuse him. He was so desperate for the game to continue that I couldn't bear to be the one to call it off, to take my bat and ball and go home. This way it was a shared, negotiated ending. Anyway, to be perfectly honest, I felt reluctant to give up myself. What I had said to Kiffo about the sense of waste wasn't just words. I felt it acutely. That there was something shameful in surrender. Just one more go? I had little to lose, particularly since it was extremely unlikely that the Ferret could dob me in to the police for stalking after just one day. And maybe, just maybe . . .

'All right, Kiffo. Saturday. But that's it.'

Kiffo beamed. I had rarely seen him look so pleased about anything. He was lonely too. He needed the warmth of shared experience.

'I'll pick you up, Saturday morning, at eight,' he said, looking like he wanted to hug me.

Chapter 21

One last go

Mum left the house at seven on Saturdays, so I was showered and ready by a quarter to eight. I had had a day to think about things and I was feeling excited as I got dressed. Something would happen today. And if it didn't, at least it would signal a finish. One way or another, this was going to be an important day.

Kiffo knocked on the door right on nine o'clock. I opened up and did a double take. He was dressed in leathers and had a crash helmet on. The only way I could tell it was him was a tell-tale tuft of red hair poking out the side of the helmet and the shape of the leather trouser legs which curved away from each other alarmingly. Kiffo couldn't stop a pig in an alley. In his right hand, he carried a spare helmet. He stood for a moment, allowing me to take in his full splendour, and then flipped up his visor in triumph.

'Surprise!'

I looked over his shoulder. Parked outside the house was a very large red motorbike. Now don't expect me to get technical here. I've no idea what type of an engine it had. No idea if it was two stroke, four stroke or breast stroke. It could have been fuelled by coal for all I know. Nor do I know if it was a Yamaha, a Mitsubishi or a Mount Fujiyama. It's best in these matters to stick to what you know. I know that it was red. And big.

Kiffo unbuckled his helmet and took it off. He really did look ridiculously pleased with himself. It was kind of disarming. I mean, he looked like a complete loser and, in other circumstances, I wouldn't have hesitated in telling him so. But right now I didn't have the heart.

OK, call me stupid if you like, but it took a few moments before the significance of the second helmet hit home.

'Kiffo,' I said, 'you aren't expecting me to get on that bike, are you?'

He looked instantly crushed.

'Well, yeah,' he said. 'I borrowed it specially. You know, get around quickly and that.'

'You can forget it.'

He grabbed my arm.

'Aw, come on, Calma. Don't be such a wuss. Look, what are we supposed to do? Grab a number 5 bus and ask the driver to follow the small guy in the business suit? Come on, Calma. Be reasonable.'

I could see his point, but I was far from convinced. There were a few little objections that sprang to mind.

'And the fact that you haven't got a licence, Kiffo? That it isn't your bike?' A sudden thought occurred to me. 'It's not stolen, is it?'

Kiffo looked horrified, as if the thought of taking something that didn't belong to him was deeply offensive to his sense of morality.

'No, it isn't,' he said, his voice thick with righteous indignation. 'It's a mate's bike. He knows I've got it!'

'All right,' I said. 'But that still doesn't mean you can legally take it out on the road. Come on, Kiffo. What if there's an accident? What if the police stop us?'

'What if, what if! Give it a break, willya? We haven't got time for this.'

'What do you mean?'

'I mean I know where he is! I'm already on the trail, Calma. I have been since seven this morning. But I tell ya. If we don't get moving soon, he'll have gone. Come on. I'm a good rider, honest. I've been on bikes since I was seven. There's nothing to worry about.'

As far as I could see, there was plenty to worry about. I had visions of a police car pulling us over, Constable Ryan getting out of the driver's side and walking towards us. Or being hit by a road train and ending up as road pizza. And for what? Just so we could spend a day following an innocent businessman around? No. The whole idea was absurd, impossible. There was no way I was getting on the back of that thing.

'All right,' I said. 'But you'd better drive slowly, OK?'

Kiffo grinned. I took the helmet and he showed me how to put it on. I checked myself out in the mirror and I have to confess that I looked pretty damn good. Sort of cool and tough. It was comforting, also, to know that with the visor down, there was little likelihood of anyone recognising me. Listen, to tell you the absolute truth, the whole idea was quite exciting! I got on the back of the bike, planted my feet firmly on the footrests and grabbed hold of Kiffo round the waist. I was ready.

I wasn't ready. For one thing, when Kiffo started the bike up it felt like there was a small earthquake under my backside. It was like sitting on top of the Space Shuttle. For another thing, when Kiffo let out the clutch we shot away like crap off a stainless steel shovel. I could feel my feet rise off the pedals. I had to struggle, pulling at Kiffo's waist, before I could stop my legs tilting towards the sky in an absurdly undignified fashion.

Even though we had been travelling for about one-point-two seconds all my muscles had locked up. I could feel my fingers digging into Kiffo's leather jacket with such intensity that it would have taken a cold chisel to loosen my grip. The wind tore at my clothing and I could see the tarmac blurring past under my feet. I risked taking a peep over Kiffo's shoulder and then wished I hadn't.

At the end of my street there is a sharp bend to the right.

We were approaching this at what seemed like two hundred kilometres an hour. Suddenly Kiffo leaned to his right and the bike tilted at an impossible angle. There was only one thing to do. If Kiffo was determined to hurl us to the ground then I must compensate. That's common sense, right? And, if I remember my physics classes correctly, in perfect keeping with one of those laws that Newton used to formulate for the sole purpose of making schoolkids' lives a misery. So I leaned sharply to my left.

Three things happened. Firstly, the bike wobbled crazily, an event that did nothing for the already fragile state of my bowels. Secondly, Kiffo started swearing in a fashion and at a volume that surprised even me. Thirdly, we slowed and then stopped. Well, how was I to know that when you went round a bend on a motorbike you were supposed to lean into it? I tried to point this out to Kiffo after he had calmed down, but I didn't get the chance. I had the first two words of a sarcastic retort framed when he screamed off and I went through the whole business of the tilting legs again.

Credit where credit is due. Kiffo knew how to handle the bike. He seemed confident in traffic and, once I had forced myself to lean with him round bends, I began to relax a little. Only a little, mind. My fingers still felt as if they had been set in quick-drying concrete, but at least my bottom was no longer trying to eat the seat upholstery. In fact, after a while, I began to enjoy myself. I even felt a sense of freedom, particularly when we were travelling down broad main streets. I could feel the wind whipping at my neck and shoulders. It was so refreshing I thought it would be nice to lift the visor up on my helmet and let the air get to my face.

Unfortunately, no sooner had I done so than a small insect, clearly suffering from acute depression, decided that my open mouth was the ideal route for a suicide mission. With kamikaze-like determination it rocketed down my throat and splattered against my tonsils. Have you ever tried to cough up your oesophagus while travelling at over sixty kilometres an hour, with the wind rushing down your throat? Trust me on this one. It's difficult.

I suppose it had one benefit, however. I was so busy trying to get rid of the insect that I had no chance to see Kiffo's road manoeuvring. All I was aware of was the bike swerving from side to side and cars flashing past me to the right and the left. By the time I had recovered and got the visor back down, we were slowing down on a quiet residential street. Actually, a rather familiar residential street. In fact, a totally bloody familiar residential street. It was with a sense of rising desperation that I found my voice as we came to a stop under my casuarina tree.

'Just what the bloody hell do you think you are doing, Kiffo?'

Kiffo pushed his visor back.

'It's the Pit Bull's place.'

'I *know* it's the Pit Bull's place! I have every reason to know where we are. What I want to know is what we are doing here!'

'He's in there. The Ferret. That's his car in the driveway. I followed him this morning and he came here. Parked up, so I figured they wouldn't be leaving immediately. Took the chance that I would have enough time to pick you up.'

I felt like screaming and beating him round the back of the head with my crash helmet. In fact, I *did* start beating him around the back of the head with my helmet.

'You bastard, Kiffo. You complete bastard! You knew I wouldn't come if I knew that this is where we would end up. The one place I swore I would never come back to. What are you trying to do? Get me in jail? Let's leave. Now.'

Kiffo did his conjuring trick with a rollie and blew a plume of smoke into the air.

'Yeah. I knew you wouldn't come, so I didn't tell you. But I didn't lie to you, Calma. I just told you I knew where the Ferret was. And I do. He's in there with the Pit Bull. Relax. There's no way she'll recognise you in that helmet. So stop hitting me with it and put it on, eh? Stay cool. Anyway, it's pretty interesting that he came here so early on a Saturday morning.'

'I'll tell you what would be pretty interesting, Kiffo. My foot disappearing up your arse. Now, for God's sake . . .'

But I didn't get any further. The front door of the Pit Bull's house opened and she and the Ferret walked out to the car. They seemed in a hurry. I scrambled to get my helmet back on and Kiffo kicked the bike into life. The car, a beautiful sleek black job – might have been a BMW, but I'm not crash hot on cars either – reversed down the driveway and swept off down the road. The occupants didn't even look in our direction.

Kiffo spun the bike round and we accelerated smoothly after the car, which made a right turn at the end of the street. The anger I was feeling started to dissolve and that sense of excitement infected me again. Maybe Kiffo was right. There probably was little chance of them seeing us. To hell with it. Let me be honest here. I really was doing this only for Kiffo. I knew, after what Jonno had told us, that there was nothing in the way of a mystery left. But we needed to see this through. Just this one last day. Anyway, this whole thing was like a movie. A car chase. Bloody oath. It was the only thing missing from our little fantasy and here was the chance to live it. All we needed was to be in radio contact with a helicopter and it would have been perfect.

> **'Roger, Foxtrot Tango One. We have visual on the target. Confirm. We have visual.'**
> **'Roger that, Delta. Proceed down Main Street on a one-zero-three.'**

It didn't really matter that we were just following a doctor and a drug counsellor, probably on their way to a drug rehabilitation meeting or something. I still got an adrenalin rush.

Kiffo caught up with the car quickly and then dropped back a little, keeping a few car lengths between us and them. Traffic was still light and we had no trouble keeping them in view. The only problem was that there were so few cars on the road that I felt we must be really conspicuous. I had to tell myself that innocent people wouldn't ever think that someone might be following them, that a motorbike in the rear-view mirror would scarcely cause anyone to panic. Still felt strange, though.

After about five minutes it was clear that the route we were following was taking us out of the city. I could only hope that they weren't going interstate. I had visions of us following them through the outback for days.

Further along, we hit heavier traffic and it was easier to stay hidden behind cars. Kiffo said something to me over his shoulder but the wind swept the words away. I tapped him on the back and yelled 'What?' into the side of his helmet. He turned his head more acutely.

'I think they might have spotted us,' he yelled. 'Look how he's slowed down.'

It was true. Before, we had been going at about eighty, but now the car had slowed to just over sixty. Of course, it probably had something to do with the increased traffic, though most other cars were still going at speeds in excess of ours. Perhaps they were just enjoying the view. We were edging closer and closer to the rear of the car now and I could make out, through the tinted windows, the bulky silhouette of the

Pit Bull. She might have been looking behind her. I couldn't be sure. Even now, I'm not sure.

What happened next wasn't in doubt, though. The car suddenly jumped forward as if something had been injected into its exhaust. It went from about sixty to one hundred in a matter of seconds. One moment we were tootling along a couple of car lengths behind, the next moment the car was dwindling to a speck in the distance. Kiffo twisted his wrist and the bike surged forward. Once again, I felt that familiar force trying to push me off the back of the bike. I glanced at the speedometer and was alarmed to see the dial creep over the one hundred mark and continue to rise. We were flashing past other vehicles now, but the black car wasn't getting any closer. We seemed to have stopped it increasing its distance from us, but we weren't making much of an inroad in decreasing the gap. I wanted to yell into Kiffo's ear, tell him to stop, that it wasn't worth getting ourselves killed for something so stupid as catching up, but I doubted he would have heard me. Even if he had, I knew that he wouldn't stop. It's that old macho crap, I guess.

We were on a long straight section of the highway, but pretty soon the road started to curve. Kiffo barely slowed down as we approached the bend. He threw himself first to one side and then the other. I gritted my teeth and hung on grimly, keeping my body moulded to his as we cornered. The rushing tarmac seemed millimetres from my trailing knee and

I had visions of us both being scraped across the road. But we were getting closer to the car. There could be no doubt that the bends were favouring us. Then we hit another straight that led up to a roundabout. I could see the brake lights of the cars in the distance as they slowed. The Ferret's car barely braked at all, just a flicker of lights as it swept round the roundabout and continued straight on. Kiffo took the inside lane, swerving on to the bicycle path on the inside of the short queue of cars. We both glanced to the right, saw that the way was clear and Kiffo accelerated into the roundabout.

It was then that I noticed the white car on our left. It was coming up to the junction to join the roundabout and I knew, I don't know how, that it wasn't going to stop. There was something about it that screamed danger. I could almost follow the driver's movements as he or she came up to the give-way sign. Look to the right. Everything clear. No sign of any traffic. Not even a large red motorbike accelerating rapidly round the inside lane. Just looking for cars. If it's not a car, can't see it. Foot on the accelerator. Pull out.

Kiffo reacted quickly, but there was nothing he could do. He tried to swerve around the front of the car, but in those few long seconds I knew that we were going to hit. I could see the face of the driver then. It was a woman and her eyes were widening in horror. I could hear her thoughts. *Where did that come from? That wasn't there a moment ago.* Her mouth was turned down, so that she looked irritated. I could see her knuckles whiten on the steering wheel and her arms bunch as she slammed her foot on the brake. The car nearly stood on end. I was aware of the screech of brakes, a smell of burning rubber and then a jolt and a crunch of metal.

NOVEMBER: Primary school, Year 6.

You sit in a corner of the school yard. Your head is slumped on your knees and you sob so much that it feels like your body is tearing itself apart. In your head are images. You see yourself sitting on the stairs, late at night, hands over your ears. Shouting comes from a room beneath you. Something smashes. There is a whole sea of pain and you sit on the seawall, letting the waves wash over you. A door opens and slams. Your father, drunk with anger, crashes past you and into his bedroom. Your mother stands at the foot of the stairs, look-ing at you. Her face is twisted as if something dark is forcing itself through. Her eyes are red, marinaded in misery.

It is the last time you see your father.

You feel a hand on your knee. You lift your head and it is the red-haired boy.

'Are you OK?' he says, gently.

You put your head on to his shoulder.

Chapter 22

Picking up the pieces

I was told later that I cleared the bonnet of the car by about two metres and then slid along the grass for another twenty before coming to rest. I have no recollection of it. All I can remember is the sense of falling, a swirl of sky and grass and the not unpleasant thought that I was going to die. It's strange. When I was on the bike, I was so tense that you could have stuck a pin in me and it wouldn't have broken the skin. Once I was off it, in the air, I felt relaxed. Liquid, almost. Maybe that's what saved me. When I got to my feet, and that was almost instantly according to witnesses, I wasn't aware of any pain. I felt fine. It was only later that I found that my legs and arms had friction burns, but even they weren't bad and disappeared after a few days. My jeans and top were never going to be the same, though. I reckon they took the main force. If we'd been going much faster, if Kiffo hadn't braked so violently, then they couldn't have absorbed the impact. I doubt if there would have been too much flesh left on my right side if we'd been going an extra ten k.

But all of those thoughts came later. I was running to find Kiffo. He lay at the side of the road about fifteen metres away. It was bizarre that, on impact, we had shot off in entirely different directions. I guess a scientist, armed with rates of trajectory, angles of impact and all that, would probably have explained it logically. I didn't care. The only thing I could focus on was Kiffo's small, inert shape. Other cars had stopped by now and people were converging on him. I saw someone talking into a mobile phone. I pushed past the gathering knot and flung myself down at his side. A sudden terror came over me then as I reached out a hand towards him. He was lying with his face away from me and I was scared about what I'd see when I turned him over. My fingers were brushing his jacket when he gave a big shudder and turned to face me. I looked into his eyes and they seemed clear. There was no sign of blood.

'Bugger me,' said Kiffo. 'Bloody women drivers!'

I was so relieved that I almost burst into tears. I could feel them prickling up behind my eyes. Instead I burst out laughing.

'It's all very well for you to laugh,' said Kiffo indignantly, 'but that bloody woman nearly killed us!' He sat bolt upright. 'Oh, shit, the bike!'

I think the conventional wisdom when dealing with accident victims is to keep them quiet, preferably motionless, until medical help arrives. Conventional wisdom, however, didn't have to deal with Kiffo. He was up on his feet and shoving his way through the crowd of onlookers before I could do anything at all. I followed.

He looked around and spotted the wreck of the bike about thirty metres away. As he ran towards it, I noticed that he was limping a bit and that one leg of his leather trousers was torn. There was a patch of what might have been blood on his left thigh. I caught up with him as he fell to his knees in front of the bike.

'Oh shit,' he said. 'Look at it!'

I looked at it. Now, as you know, I am by no means an expert in the field of motor mechanics, but I could see instantly that it was not in what you'd call showroom condition. There were a few clues that I followed here. Firstly, the engine was at an angle that I suspected was a far cry from the original engineer's intentions. When Kiffo touched it, something fell off with a dull thunk. It might have been the carburettor, it might have been the gearbox. Like I said, I'm not an expert. Secondly, as far as the bodywork was concerned, it was still red. But it was also in about a thousand pieces, scattered over at least thirty square metres. One wheel was bent almost at right angles to itself. Interestingly, the only thing that seemed to be undamaged was the headlamp. It was still rolling gently at the side of the road. I thought about pointing it out to Kiffo, but then reconsidered. I guessed it wouldn't exactly lift his spirits.

We sat on the side of the road until the ambulance and the police arrived. Kiffo seemed to be in shock, either from the accident or the certain knowledge that he owed some friend of his a considerable sum of money. I kept my arm around him, but he didn't seem to notice. He just stared at the bike and groaned. I took the opportunity to look at his leg. There was a ragged tear in the leg of his leather pants, surrounded by blood. I was relieved to see that there didn't appear to be any fresh flow, but I couldn't tell how badly he was injured. Considering what had happened, it was a miracle that we had got off so lightly.

A couple of people came up and asked if we were all right and I assured them we were fine. I was surprised at how calm I felt and how my voice didn't even tremble. Even the thought that I was going to be in trouble with the police didn't faze me too much. Before the accident, I would have been in panic at the prospect. Now, it seemed an irrelevance somehow. Being alive – that was the important thing. Everything else was secondary.

I noticed, briefly, the woman who had been driving the white car. She was leaning over by the side of the road, throwing up. A couple of people were attending to her. I remember thinking how strange it was that she should be physically sick when Kiffo and I were basically OK. After all, she had been protected by her car. We had nothing. Of course, I knew some-where at the back of my mind that the shock was only delayed, that it would kick in later. But just then, sitting on the grass with my arm around Kiffo, it all seemed tranquil. Right, somehow.

What happened next remains sort of blurry. I remember the flashing lights and being helped into an ambulance with Kiffo and the woman from the car. There were police around, but they didn't bother us much. They were more concerned with the wreckage and the line of cars that had formed on all sides of the roundabout. I supposed that they would be com-ing to see us at the hospital later, once they had sorted out this mess. It didn't seem important. I remember very little about the actual journey to the hospital. I think the woman was cry-ing. Kiffo was just silent, lost in his thoughts about the bike.

We were taken to the casualty department at the hospital and checked over. I remember that there were X-rays and a number of examinations by a series of doctors. One, a rather gorgeous guy who looked about twenty, smiled at me and said, 'You look in pretty good shape to me.' I blushed. I still don't know whether he was making a medical judgement or flirting.

After a while, I was taken to a waiting area and found myself sitting next to the driver of the car. She was really sweet. I didn't have to say anything about it being her fault. Not that I would. Blame seemed irrelevant. But she was still crying and apologising, saying that she hadn't seen us at all, that she could have killed us, that she had a granddaughter a little older than me and when she thought of what might have happened, she doubted if she would ever forgive herself. I found myself in the strange situation of comforting her, telling her that an accident can happen to anyone, that it wasn't anyone's fault, even though I knew it was hers. I felt sorry for her.

Sometime later, a nurse came and took her away and I was left alone. Then a doctor told me that the police were waiting to interview me and that my mother had been notified. He said they still wanted to run a few tests, so the police would have to wait. I wouldn't swear to it, but he seemed pleased at keeping the police waiting. Finally, Kiffo was brought out in a wheelchair, which worried me until the nurse explained that there was nothing major wrong, just a gash that had been stitched. The wheelchair was to help take the weight off for a while. I smiled at Kiffo.

'Wassup, Kiffo?' I said.

'Wassup, Calma?' he replied.

I was relieved that he was in a pretty good emotional state. Maybe the hours of tests and X-rays and stitches had given him time to reach my perspective, that nothing else really mattered other than the fact that we were alive.

'So what happens now?' he asked.

'I dunno. I guess we'll get interviewed by the police and at some stage they'll let us go home . . .'

'No. I mean about the Pit Bull.'

'What are you on about, Kiffo?'

He leaned urgently towards me and lowered his voice, even though we were completely alone.

'You don't really think that was an accident, do you?'

I felt like smacking him around the face then. Instead, I resorted to my old favourite – sarcasm.

'No, of course not, Kiffo. Just because it was clearly an accident, and about fifty people could testify to it being an accident, doesn't mean I'm not suspicious. It's all a conspiracy organised by the Pit Bull!'

Kiffo nodded.

'I'm glad you think so. I thought you might have been fooled.'

I felt like screaming. Instead I rolled my eyes as Kiffo continued.

'It's obvious that they spotted us. That's why the Ferret slowed down and then took off at that speed. I reckon that he had a phone with him and rang his accomplice, the woman in the white car. Her orders were to take us out. We were too close to them, Calma. We were a threat that needed eliminating.'

Maybe I should have humoured him. It was clear that nothing was going to deflect Kiffo from his theory, certainly not facts or reality. But I couldn't let it go.

'Kiffo, listen,' I said. 'It was an accident, pure and simple.

Get that through your head. I talked to the woman in the car. She's got white hair, a touch of arthritis and a grandchild about our age. She was so upset that she was vomiting and crying at the same time. She's not a geriatric hit woman, for God's sake! It's over, Kiffo. Finished.'

It was his turn to roll his eyes now.

'Don't take that attitude with me, Kiffo! It's not my fault that you have a problem facing up to the real world, that you're lost in your own little fantasy. Well, I've had enough of it.'

But Kiffo was still rolling his eyes. I could see nothing but the whites. And he was twitching, like an electric current was going through him. I heard a scream and I suppose it must have been mine. Then there was a whole bunch of people in white and a lot of shouting and yelling. Someone dragged me to my feet and bustled me out of the room. The last I saw of Kiffo was a glimpse of red hair beneath a tide of white uniforms.

Chapter 23

Not to praise him

I stopped off at the Adult shop on my way to the funeral.

Everyone else went by car or by bus. I walked.

It was a blazing hot day. Even at nine in the morning the heat was solid. The sky was cloudless, and tarmac sparkled in black pools. Within five minutes, I was bathed in sweat. I could feel droplets gathering under my tank top and running down my stomach and sides. I could feel a damp stain growing in the waistband of my shorts.

Mum had offered to drive me but I just felt like walking. I don't think it was one of those grand emotional gestures or anything. Who can tell? I suppose that any other form of transport would have cut out the visit to the Adult shop, but I swear that I had nothing specific planned, despite any evidence to the contrary. Let's be honest. I wasn't thinking clearly. I felt sick and dizzy even before the sun worked on me.

Everything had the blurry edges of a dream.

I can't remember any details of the walk, except for the constant fist of heat. But I did some thinking. I remember thinking that they had got it right in films. Funerals should be in driving rain. There should be a huddled knot of mourners around an open grave. Women should hug small, grim-faced children to them. A priest should crumble earth over the grave and there should be a mysterious stranger standing off to one side. Kiffo's funeral was to take place in the airconditioning of the Methodist Church. We were to sit in rows on comfortable chairs. There would be a public address system.

I had been told in great detail what would happen. We had rehearsed it at school, like a play. And I suppose that's what it was, a dramatic performance in which we all had our roles. Even the stage had been carefully managed. Kiffo wasn't religious. But the school had arranged everything, including the booking of the Church. Yes, everyone had gone to great lengths to make sure that it all went off well, that the show was flawless. I guess I let them down.

I remember thinking about my own body as I was walking. Sweat was dripping into my eyes and making them sting. Whatever I looked at was tinged with a milky sheen. The sun made my arms and legs tingle. I could feel chemical reactions going off, like little bombs, all along my skin. Cause and effect. Like Kiffo's death. Someone – I can't remember who – told me that Kiffo had died from an embolism. A little clot of blood, no bigger than a baby's fingernail, had formed when he had been hit by the car. Or when he hit the ground. It had stayed there for a while and then, released into his bloodstream, travelled like a missile to the brain. Boom! Gone. It was a freak occurrence. Any kind of trauma could manufacture this little bullet and set it speeding towards its target. Nothing anyone could do.

I almost hated Kiffo for that. Something so silly, so undramatic, so childish. How could he have let it happen? It felt fragile, this business of living. An accident that could fold up on itself at any moment. I brushed the sweat out of my eyes, but they filled up again almost immediately.

When I reached the church, everyone else was already there. People milled around outside, finding shade wherever they could. The Principal moved amongst the small crowd, chatting briefly with everyone and wearing an air of solemnity like an ill-fitting suit.

Kiffo's dad was there. For a moment I didn't recognise him, but then I realised he had shaved. Normally he wore a thick stubble continuously, but now his face was blotched with the violence of the razor. It looked like a potato. His eyes moved constantly and his fingers clenched and relaxed all the time. It was as if a drink lay somewhere just beyond his sight and the effort of finding it was making him flinch.

I didn't know many of the people there. A couple of teachers, some rellies. Maybe a neighbour or two. Jonno wasn't there. I spotted a few of the kids from my class. Melanie Simpson, Rachael Smith, Natalie Sykes, Nathan Manning, Vanessa Aldrick. They stood around, looking embarrassed. Vanessa, for once, didn't seem bored. I suppose that might have been too difficult to manage, under the circumstances, even for her. I walked slowly to the doors of the church and joined the strange assembly. I didn't know what else to do. The Principal dutifully made his way towards me.

'Are you all right, Calma?' he asked in the tone he reserved for occasions when he wanted to be seen as caring and sensitive. I noticed that he gave me a quick look up and down, taking in my sodden clothes and limp, drenched hair. His eyes showed a flash of irritation. I had not dressed the part. I was letting the side down. But then his eyes closed down again and concern struggled to the surface once more.

'You seem a little distraught. Are you sure that you are up to this, Calma?'

I simply nodded. It was too much effort to talk. Luckily, the Principal saw someone he wanted to speak to and hurried off.

I looked at the church doors and wondered why we were locked outside. Had someone forgotten the keys? Was there an opening time, like a pub? I had images of a priest inside the cool church looking at his watch, waiting for the second hand to sweep past the hour before he would open up and let us in, the great church-going public thirsty for God. Even as these ideas were going through my mind, the doors opened and I realised what was going on. There was another funeral taking place in there. People filed out, shaking the hand of the priest or whoever it was, muttering a few words before they made for the car park. Some walked briskly, clearly relieved to be out of there. Others walked slowly, bent with grief or exhaustion. I saw a woman being supported by someone who might have been her son. She looked puzzled, but only faintly, like this was a problem that had touched her briefly before being dismissed as beyond her understanding. It was almost like a revelation. I saw that she was in a situation where things had happened to her but they made little sense, exhibited no logic. The death she was there for had forced itself on her. Since then, the world had forced other things – funeral, flowers, arrangements, insurance, who knows – and these were things that happened also. They happened without her. She was powerless. I felt the same.

Within minutes they had all disappeared, taking their world with them. It was our turn. The priest shook the Principal's hand and spoke quietly, presumably an apology for the lateness. We filed into the church. It seemed tinged with other people's sadness. I took up my position in the front pew. We had rehearsed all this. As one of the speakers, I had to be in the right position, waiting for my cue. The school had asked me to say a few words, you see. After the Principal, of course. I was going to be the last to speak and was stuck on the outside of the row.

We made a small congregation. I looked around as we waited for the ceremony to start. The church was big. The airconditioning made my skin prickle. Hot sweat was battling it out with the chilly atmosphere. I could feel my wet tank top crinkle. I could sense it drying.

The front row was filled with people from the school. The rellies, or whoever they were, had been stuck in the rows behind. With the exception of Kiffo's dad, of course. He was in the front row next to the Principal, as if the school had done him a big favour, giving him a ringside seat. Letting him in on the show of his son's funeral, like it was a special privilege. I noticed the Principal patting him on the arm, but Kiffo's dad wore a haunted look. He wanted to be down the pub where at least he knew people, where it was a familiar world, not this strange, alien place run by people he didn't know and couldn't understand. His hands trembled.

Then I noticed Kiffo's casket. It was already in place at the side of the pulpit. It was so bizarre, so strange and sad. I had an overwhelming urge to check inside it, to see if Kiffo was really there. It didn't seem likely to me. This wasn't the sort of place Kiffo would be seen dead in. He would have hated this. The lights were too bright, for one thing. And it was too quiet.

The priest climbed up the few steps to the pulpit and looked down at the small gathering. For a moment, I had this wild idea that he was going to start off a stand-up comedy routine. You know, 'My wife is so ugly that when she was born the midwife smacked her mother . . .' It was all I could do to stop from laughing.

We sang a few hymns, none of them appropriate. If I'd been running the show, I'd have at least chosen a couple of rap songs. Kiffo liked rap. When we had finished singing we all sat down again and the priest composed his features. You could tell that he had done this a thousand times before. He looked over us for a few moments and then he started to speak.

'We are here today to say goodbye to Jaryd Kiffing and, if I may say so, to celebrate his life, tragically short though that may have been. Jaryd was taken from us quickly and unexpectedly. He was a boy who was full of life. He had a bright future in front of him . . .'

I couldn't help it. I started thinking, what if Kiffo had a bright future *behind* him? Did I have a bright past ahead of me, or a bright present in front and behind? It's easy to get off track in circumstances like this, so I tried to re-focus.

'. . . and yet he was cut down before he had time to bloom and flourish. It is at times like this that we ask ourselves: *Why? Why Jaryd Kiffing?* He was no more than a child. He was innocent. And yet he was taken from us without explanation. It is not surprising that under circumstances like this we tend to doubt. Yes, we doubt the God that seems so capricious. I have encountered this doubt many times, from grieving parents like William here . . .'

I had no idea who he was talking about. It took a few seconds to register that he was referring to Kiffo's dad. By the time I was back up to speed I had missed a bit.

'. . . that there *is* a reason, though it might be beyond our comprehension. The Bible tells us that there is a special providence in the fall of a sparrow. And if a sparrow falls, how much more significance is there in the fall of Jaryd, who was loved by family and friends and, of course, by God?'

I started to zone out again at around this point. I was developing a dull headache, the legacy of my walk in the heat, I suppose. Anyway, the words started to melt into each other. I caught the odd phrase, the occasional reference to 'Jaryd' and each time he said it, the stab of pain in my head increased. I wasn't angry, you understand. I wasn't full of indignation, as some people suggested later. I just felt tired and *irritated*. I was irritated by the priest's refusal to call him 'Kiffo'. Couldn't he have done his research? I mean, everyone called him Kiffo. Most of the teachers called him Kiffo. Even the Pit Bull had called him Kiffo.

I wasn't even aware that he had finished. I remember looking up and seeing the Principal on the pulpit. The switch had passed me by, like a conjuring trick.

I forced myself to focus again. For some reason, I wanted to hear what he had to say.

'. . . will be remembered by all his friends and by all the staff with considerable fondness. He was a larrikin in the great

Australian spirit. But he was a student with considerable potential. He had much to offer and it is a cruel blow that he was taken from us before we had the opportunity to see him develop into the fine adult that he would undoubtedly have become. For there is no doubt that he enriched the lives of all he came into contact with. We will miss him deeply. I can only say that his spirit lives on in all of us, that though he has gone, there will always be a part of Jaryd Kiffing that stays with us. I sense him here with us now. God bless, Jaryd. God speed. Thank you.'

He got down from the pulpit as if expecting the round of applause that his final comment seemed to invite. It must have been a good speech. I noticed Mrs Mills (why hadn't I seen her before?) sniffling quietly into her handkerchief. The Principal moved smartly and put a comforting arm around her shoulder. Yes, it must have been a very good speech.

The priest ascended the pulpit once more. I was getting tired of the bobbing up and down. He stood for a few moments, like someone moved to profound contemplation.

'Thank you, Mr Di Matteo. I am sure everyone is as moved as I am by your wonderful tribute to this fine young man.'

The Principal graciously lowered his head in acknowledgement of the compliment and the priest carried on.

'Our last speaker is someone who knew Jaryd very well. A close friend who was with him at the time of the tragic accident. Someone who is admirably qualified to tell us about Jaryd, what he meant to her and what he meant to the rest of his friends. Calma Harrison.'

It was like an introduction in some cheap floor show. 'Give it up, ladies and gentlemen, for your friend and mine . . .'

> *Thank you very much, ladies and gentlemen. Thank you. It's great to be here today. So Kiffo goes into a bar and the bartender, he says to him, 'Kiffo, there was this great lump of tarmac in here and he was looking for you. Didn't look too pleased with you, mate!' And Kiffo goes pale and says, 'I'm not fighting him. I know him. He's a complete cycle path.' Thanks. Thanks a lot. My name's Calma Harrison and you've been a great audience.*

I got to my feet and moved towards the pulpit. I kept my hands in my pockets. The priest was smiling. He held out a hand and took my arm, guiding me up the steps. After enquiring if I was 'up to it' he glided away.

I looked briefly at the congregation and began. My voice was a little quiet, but you had to admit that the PA system was good.

'Ladies and gentlemen. There has been much said today about Kiffo. In particular, I want to focus on one statement from our Principal, Mr Di Matteo. He said that Jaryd enriched the lives of all who knew him. That's certainly true of me, but I would suggest that many others would disagree. They might argue that he actually *impoverished* their lives. To the tune of

TVs, video recorders, computer equipment, stereo systems, DVDs and other sundry personal items. Let's be honest, ladies and gentlemen, he did have a marked inclination to break into people's homes. And if something wasn't nailed down, he would have it.'

I paused here for dramatic effect, and to watch the reaction of my audience. Kiffo's dad was leaning forward slightly in his pew, hands plucking nervously at each other. He was taking in nothing at all. The wheel was spinning, it would appear, but the hamster was dead. Among the others, though, there was a distinct stir. People were shaking their heads slightly as if they distrusted the evidence of their own ears. Like giving the TV a bit of a thump, they seemed to be under the impression that a quick shake of the head would improve the reception. Mr Di Matteo's reaction was the best, however. He wore the bewildered expression of someone who had just been beaten, violently and unexpectedly, around the back of the head with a piece of lead piping. His mouth hung open a little and his eyes were glassy. I smiled sweetly and continued.

'Yes, Kiffo was not exactly a saint. Not when he was alive and certainly not now he's dead. Call me old-fashioned, but I don't believe that a person's character changes simply because he has stopped breathing. Do you want to hear the truth about Kiffo?'

Judging by the head-shaking out there, the general opinion seemed to be, 'No thanks, if it's all the same to you.' Certainly the mourners were getting restless at this point. In fact, the Principal seemed distinctly angry. He turned quickly towards Mrs Mills, who had the expression of someone who had had a cattle prod administered to her rectum. And then the Principal was on his feet and moving towards the pulpit. Like a superhero, he was leaping into action to save the situation. And there was only one way to do that – to forcibly remove me. All he needed was his jocks on the outside and he would really have looked the part. Complete and utter dickhead though he undoubtedly was, he nonetheless had the strength and the authority to do it. So I put Plan B into action.

Reaching quickly into my pocket, I removed the fluffy pink handcuffs that I had purchased earlier at the Adult shop. Thirty-five dollars and fifty cents' worth of kitsch bondage gear. With a fluency that surprised me, I slapped one cuff around my left wrist and the other around the brass rail of the pulpit. That stopped him. Whether it was the sight of one of his Year 10 students manacled to a religious icon with something that was more at home in the Sydney Mardi Gras, or simply that he recognised the futility of any further action, I cannot say. But he stopped in his tracks. I looked him squarely in the eye.

'Please sit down, Mr Di Matteo. Sit down NOW!'

And he did. Possibly he understood that I had him by the short ones. Unless he had a pair of bolt cutters tucked into an inside pocket, I was staying attached to the pulpit for the foreseeable future. No one else moved.

'The truth about Kiffo?' I continued. 'It's a difficult one. Someone once said that the first casualty of war is the truth. And Kiffo's life was a war zone, so I guess I shouldn't be too surprised to hear the offensive horseshit that's been offered up to this point. Come on, people. Let's be honest. None of you liked Kiffo. The "grieving father" least of all. Kiffo didn't tell me much about you, Mr Kiffing, but he didn't need to. I could see it in his eyes and the bruises that he did his best to conceal. I'm not a psychoanalyst, but I do know that a lot of the anger that Kiffo carried around with him, the hatred of authority figures, his tendency towards mindless violence, had to have their roots in your treatment of him. Some of his worst characteristics were those that you taught him.'

Boy, I had their attention now. The congregation sat still, eyes fixed and glassy. They looked like a whole bunch of rabbits caught in a powerful headlight. Part of me wondered why they didn't just leave. I suppose that would have stopped me. Made me look a bit foolish as well, handcuffed to a pulpit in an empty church with just a coffin for company. I honestly don't think it occurred to them. I had them hypnotised. Mr Di Matteo's expression was still the best. I swear that he could see the big bold headlines in the local paper if news of this got out. He was a man staring at the death of his career.

'And then there was school,' I continued. 'The place where abused kids should be able to find support and understanding. So what did he get at school? A different kind of violence, that's what. A worse type of violence, if that's possible. Because his father was just beating his body, whereas the school was breaking his spirit. All the time I knew him, and I spent a lot of time with him in class, he was told that he was stupid. Stupid because he didn't know what a metaphor was. Stupid because he couldn't see why it was important to know. And if you tell someone they're stupid enough times, they will believe you. And Kiffo did believe it.'

I could feel small beads of sweat gathering on my face. Maybe the airconditioning had broken down. I brushed a damp lock of hair from my eyes and carried on.

'His teachers hated him. I don't blame them, particularly. He could be absolutely vile in class. And he was a thorn in your side, Mr Di Matteo. But he's just a larrikin now, isn't he? Because he can't answer back. Death has removed the problem and you can afford to be generous. It's easy to like the dead, Mr Di Matteo. They make so few demands.'

I paused once more. The headache was starting to kick in again and tiredness was flooding through my body. I felt on the point of collapse. My legs were starting to tremble and drops of sweat stung my eyes. My thoughts were muddy. Why was I doing this? What was it I was trying to say? When I had started out on my speech, the conclusion had been clear, a bright destination. Now, it seemed beyond my reach, like the name of someone you've forgotten. I forced myself on, in the hope that the destination would reveal itself in the process of travelling.

'And what about me? Do you know, I still don't know what Kiffo thought about me. Not really. He didn't see things the way others saw them. He knew, I suppose, that I was the best learner in the class but I don't think he was impressed by it. It was something I had that he didn't, but he placed no great importance on it. Like his red hair or his bandy legs. A characteristic – it didn't make you better or worse. An accident of birth.'

The lock of hair had crept back. I plastered it behind my ear.

'And that's what I learned from Kiffo. That underneath we are all pretty much the same, that we shouldn't judge by appearances, as he was judged his entire life. Recently, there was an unpleasant rumour about me, and, for a time, my life was hell.'

I looked at Rachael Smith in the front row. Her eyes flickered downwards.

'People avoided looking me in the eyes,' I said. 'Others just avoided me. And for a while, I knew what it must be like to inhabit Kiffo's world – a world where everyone judges you and finds you wanting. The only person who didn't do that was Kiffo. It didn't matter to him what other people thought. He accepted me. He gave me friendship and support.'

I was building up momentum again and the destination, if not sparkling clear, was at least getting less blurry around the edges. But the light-headed feeling was still there and I had to force myself to focus. I desperately wanted to sleep, but I had to get through this first.

'I have only vague notions of Kiffo's true feelings towards me. But I know how I feel. I loved Kiffo. Forty thousand brothers could not, with all their quantity of love, make up my sum. And now I find myself here with a box beside me and a mouth full of empty words. Perhaps, in the end, at the end, this is all I can do – present for him the most absurd image I can, chained to a pulpit with a tacky sex toy. And Kiffo would have loved this. He would have laughed because this is his kind of style. So come on, guys, let's have a good laugh, for Kiffo's sake. And then take that damn box away and burn it so we can get the hell out of here.'

I could feel myself going in the last couple of sentences. The light shifted and swirled. The last image I saw was the Principal leaning forward in his chair before the world tilted and crashed. And then, as it says in all the best books, there was only darkness.

DECEMBER: Primary school, Year 6.

You sit under a leafy tree in a corner of the school yard. It is breaktime and you have a school book open. Tucked within the pages, there is a newspaper clipping. You read.

An inquest is to be held after the discovery on Monday of a body in a northern suburbs townhouse. A police spokesperson confirmed that the deceased was 17 years of age and a known heroin addict. The officer declined to comment on suggestions that the death was caused by an overdose. 'Investigations are proceeding,' he said, 'but we are not actively looking for any other person in relation to this matter.'

The body was discovered late Monday afternoon by the deceased's younger brother.

You sit back as the sun splashes through the leaves above you. In your head, a fist pounds a wall as tears fall down a small boy's face. You notice, without surprise, that your cheeks are wet too.

Chapter 24

Mediation

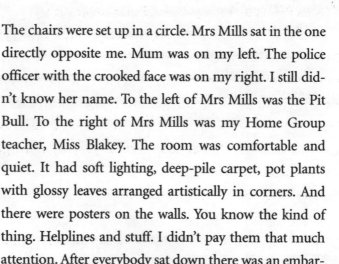

The chairs were set up in a circle. Mrs Mills sat in the one directly opposite me. Mum was on my left. The police officer with the crooked face was on my right. I still didn't know her name. To the left of Mrs Mills was the Pit Bull. To the right of Mrs Mills was my Home Group teacher, Miss Blakey. The room was comfortable and quiet. It had soft lighting, deep-pile carpet, pot plants with glossy leaves arranged artistically in corners. And there were posters on the walls. You know the kind of thing. Helplines and stuff. I didn't pay them that much attention. After everybody sat down there was an embarrassed pause, as if we realised the show had started, but no one could remember who should deliver the first line. Why was I here? The question fluttered across my mind and was gone. Mrs Mills cleared her throat.

'We are here today to engage in a process of mediation and I welcome you all. It is not the purpose of this meeting to decide who is right or who is wrong, whether people are good or bad. We are not here to allocate blame. What we *are* here to do is to repair any damage that might have been caused by recent events. As far as we can. The death of Jaryd Kiffing cannot be undone by anything we might say here. But we can start the process of healing. Calma, would you like to start? Have you anything you want to say?'

I shook my head.

'Miss Payne, perhaps you could start us off then?'

I kept my head down. I didn't want to look at anyone. There was another pause.

'I'd . . . I'd like to say that I am so, so sorry about the death of Kiffo. This is the first time, in all my years of teaching, that I've . . . lost . . . a student. And it was so sudden. I know that you cared for him, Calma. And I feel for you. My heart goes out to you. It really does.'

I looked up then. I couldn't help it.

'I don't believe you,' I said. 'You hated him.'

The Pit Bull leaned forward in her chair and fixed her eyes steadily on mine.

'I understand why you don't believe me, Calma. And maybe I don't blame you. I know how I appear to students, particularly at the beginning of a course. Trust me, I know. Horrible, nasty, strict, no sense of humour? I know. But I do care, whatever you may think. Perhaps I care too much. It would be very easy to be a popular teacher. I could make jokes, get the students to like me. You look as if you don't think that is possible, but it is. I don't do things that way, Calma. Maybe I *can't* do things that way. I get my students under control. In order to *teach* them. Only when they are under control can I relax the tight grip, give a little more freedom. Only when they are learning. It's what I am paid to do.'

'The students hate you.'

'That's actually not true, Calma.' This was Miss Blakey. 'Oh, I'm not saying that Miss Payne is the most popular teacher in the school. She isn't. But she is one of the most respected. Would it surprise you to know that Vanessa Aldrick thinks that Miss Payne is the best teacher she has ever had? That she has learned more from her in one term than in all her other terms of English? And Vanessa's not the only one. Not by a long way.'

Vanessa? Perhaps I shouldn't have been surprised. After all, the world had been making a habit recently of turning my expectations and perceptions upside down. But Vanessa?

'Think of it this way, Calma,' said the Pit Bull. 'You are talented at English. Perhaps the most talented I have ever taught. But the other kids in the class, they're not like you. I could leave you alone and you would be fine. In fact, for someone like you, it is probably better to leave you alone. But not the others. They need teaching, Calma. And that's what I do. You might not like my style. Hell, I don't like my style sometimes. But it does get results. And that, as I said before, is what I am paid to do.'

There was silence for a while. Mrs Mills broke it. God, there was something about her voice that made me want to scream. So professional, so soothing. So reasonable.

'But, in the end, it's not Miss Payne's teaching style that is at issue here, is it? It's the extra-curricular activities that occurred between you, Kiffo and her that are our main concern. Now, Calma, I know that you are going to find this difficult, but I want you to remember that no one here wishes you any harm, or wants to see you humiliated. But we need to get this out in the open. Can you tell us your suspicions about Miss Payne? What was it you and Kiffo thought she was doing?'

This was what I had been dreading. How could I say it? It sounded so stupid now, even when it was just in my head. There were all these adults around and what I was going to say would just sound so infantile to them. It sounded infantile to me. It was like I was being forced to say that I thought she was from outer space, or something. How could I, in that room, in that company, say, 'I thought you were involved in organised crime,' and retain any credibility? But I didn't know what else to do. I needed Kiffo. But he wasn't around. He was never going to be around and there wasn't anything else to do.

'I thought . . . I thought you were dealing drugs.'

'I know,' said the Pit Bull. 'And now I know what happened, I can understand just how you might have come to that conclusion. It wasn't a stupid conclusion to reach, given the circumstances.' I felt like telling her to fuck off with her patronising attitude, but I guess I wasn't in a position to do so. She continued.

'All I can do is answer your questions as fully as possible. I think you deserve that. I believe you know, now, that I am a drug counsellor in my spare time. A qualified one, by the way.'

She paused, presumably to lend the point maximum significance. I kept silent.

'You also know that I spend a lot of my time dealing with those who have dependencies, of one kind or another. Which means that very often I have to get out of my bed at ludicrous times in the morning. Drug addicts don't watch the clock, Calma. They have a different way of measuring time to the rest of us. I'm not complaining. I'm just explaining it to you. Now I know that you watched me. Followed me. And you thought it was strange that I was meeting Dr Collins at three or four in the morning. Am I right?'

I kept my eyes fixed firmly on the floor. Childish, I know, but I didn't want to give her any more satisfaction than necessary. She pushed against my silence, regardless.

'So. I am a qualified volunteer drugs counsellor. Would you say that explains my activities adequately?'

This time, I had no option but to nod sullenly. This was old stuff. I'd worked all this out for myself. With assistance from the charming Jonno, of course.

'Is there anything else you would like to ask me? Anything that you think might help? That's what this is all about. To ask questions and get answers.'

If you think about it, I didn't have anywhere to go. If I just carried on, head down, making the occasional half-hearted comment, then I was going to appear even more of a loser. There was no option but to try to keep as much dignity as I possibly could. Ask the questions. Get the answers. Anyway, there were still things that I needed to sort out in my head. Not for their benefit, but for Kiffo's and my own.

Look. I don't want to go through all of this in tedious detail. The whole thing went on for what seemed like forever. If it's OK with you, I'll summarise. The questions I put and the answers the Pit Bull gave me. It'll save us all time.

Q. Where were she and the Ferret going when Kiffo and I were following on the bike?

A. *To a conference on 'New Directions in Dependency'. Their presence was noted in the minutes. The Pit Bull was the keynote speaker. All verifiable.*

Q. Why did the car suddenly speed up?

A. *Explanation a little embarrassing. The Pit Bull's watch was running slow. They noticed, during the journey, the real*

time on the car clock and realised they were going to be late.
Hence the sudden acceleration. At no time were they aware of
being followed.

Q. Why had the Pit Bull made comments about having
dealings with the Kiffing family?

A. *Tricky, this one. Confidentiality, and all that. Suffice to say*
that in her professional capacity as a drug counsellor, she had
occasion to know about . . . the problems that a certain member
of the family had experienced in the past. She could say nothing
more about the subject. She also admitted that she regretted hav-
ing made the original remark to me, and that it bordered on
being unprofessional.

Q. What was it that the Ferret had passed to her that night?
The white stuff in the plastic bag.

A. *Naltrexone. A drug widely used in the treatment of heroin*
addiction. Available on prescription, often used as a 'rapid
detoxification agent' for addicts trying to kick the habit. Dr
Collins was a General Practitioner and therefore qualified to dis-
pense the drug. It was an emergency, though she was prepared to
admit that receiving the bag was probably a breach of acceptable
practice, since she, the Pit Bull, was not herself qualified to dis-
pense it. In the circumstances (and confidentiality prevented her
from disclosing those), the lapse of protocol would be understood
by all but the most unforgiving persons.

Look, there was other stuff. But it wasn't really very important. Mum talked. The police officer talked. Just words, after all. And right towards the end, I started to cry. I didn't want to. God knows, I didn't want to. But I couldn't stop. The funny thing is, it wasn't like real crying at all. Not gut-wrenching sobs or an overflowing of emotion. Nothing like that. It was like puking up something hard, solid, lodged in dark places I didn't know existed.

The tears flowed down my cheeks but they weren't tears of remorse. They weren't tears of humiliation, even though I knew that I had made myself look like a ten-year-old. They had nothing to do with the fact that it was:

Game over

Finished

End of story.

I'd known that for a long time really. The tears were, finally, for Kiffo. For the life that he had led and the life denied now forever. More than anything else, for the cold, hard, implacable waste of it all.

And the pity of it, Kiffo. Oh, Kiffo, the pity of it.

Chapter 25

Homophones and the world wide web

Well, there you go. The end. Or nearly so. And I guess you're expecting a final chapter that does all a final chapter should. Tying up the loose ends, that kind of thing. Listen, I don't blame you. If this were a book I was reading, rather than writing, I'd expect the same thing. So what can I tell you?

After the funeral, I suppose I was in disgrace for a while. I don't remember much of what happened after the dramatic finale to my eulogy. Someone told me later that the Prinny had to call a locksmith to get me out of those handcuffs. I wish I could have seen it. Some poor bastard came to the church with bolt cutters and then I was whipped away to the hospital. Had all kinds of tests done, and it seems it was heat exhaustion, pure and simple. I don't remember much of that either. Apparently Mum was called at work and she turned up all weeping, wailing, gnashing teeth and self-recrimination. Takes all sorts, I guess.

So they gave me a couple of weeks off school. Fortunate that, since it took me up to the four-week mid-year break. They also put out a story that I was ill and suffering from depression, that my outburst at the church was due to a combination of heat exhaustion and post-traumatic stress. And maybe that wasn't so far from the truth. The real reason, though, was that I was an embarrassment that they could do without. The school, I mean. The Prinny was undoubtedly crapping himself that I would go to the local newspaper and sell my story. Yeah, right! I mean, if you've ever read our local rag, then you'd understand that: a) they wouldn't be able to afford more than $1.25 for any exclusive; and b) they could turn any story, no matter how straightforward, into something completely incomprehensible. Kiffo couldn't make as many grammatical errors as those guys churn out as a matter of routine. Still, the Prinny was worried about headlines like 'Schoolgirl in Church Bondage Horror', so every effort was made to keep a lid on things. I suppose that's why I never heard anything from the police. Except for statements about the accident, obviously. But in relation to the alleged teacher-stalking charges, it was as if it had never happened. Maybe Constable Ryan pulled a few strings. Who knows?

Yeah, OK. There was that mediation meeting thing. I was called up at home and asked if I was prepared to take part in it. Well, what could I say? I didn't really have a choice. It would have needed more strength than I possessed to say shove it. It turned out that while I was babbling in hospital, in some kind of delirium I guess, I said all sorts of things about the Pit Bull and Kiffo and me. Blew it big time. So there they were at school, probably pissing themselves at the realisation that I had suspicions the Pit Bull was working with an organised crime cartel. It must have occurred to someone that it would be the trendy, caring kind of thing to do, to have a mediation meeting. I don't want to go on about it. I've already let you in on that nightmare. I suppose they all had a good laugh afterwards. Calma Harrison, private eye, tough chick, blubbering like a baby.

What about the Fridge? I hear you say. I bet you're hoping for a happy ending with that one. How about something like:

> *Mrs Harrison rushed to the hospital. Her face was twisted with anxiety, her coat slipped from her shoulders, revealing a worn and torn supermarket uniform. She rushed up to the nurse at reception.*
>
> *'My daughter!' she screamed. 'You have my daughter. I have to see her now!'*
>
> *'And your daughter's name, Ma'am?'*
>
> *'Calma Harrison. Hurry please.'*
>
> *'She's in room 101. But, Ma'am, you can't see her now. The doctors . . .'*
>
> *But it was too late. Mrs Harrison rushed down the corridor, elbowing terminally ill patients out of*

the way. She thrust open the door of room 101 and
stifled a sob as she saw her daughter lying on the
hospital bed, drips snaking from her thin arms. She
flung herself on the bed, tears cascading down her
face, and cradled Calma lovingly in her arms. The
girl opened her puffy eyes.

'Mum, is that you?' she sighed.

'It's me, my darling. I'm here. I'm here and I'll
never let you go again!' Mrs Harrison's body was
racked by paroxysms of sobbing as she stroked her
ailing daughter's oh so pale face.

'I love you, Mum,' the girl breathed.

'I love you too, my darling. Oh, how I love you!'

Well, close, but no cigar, I'm afraid. Actually, not all that close
when I come to think about it. Sure, we talked. Mum even took
a couple of days off work to spend time with me. But I realised
pretty quickly that she had her mind on work every moment we
were together. Kind of mentally looking at her watch. And that
sort of thing isn't exactly conducive to intimate revelations. I
don't know who was more relieved when she went back to work.
And then we drifted back into the old ways. Don't get me
wrong. Things *are* better now. We do have dinners together
when her work schedule permits. We even watch the TV for an
hour or so in the evenings *and* we chat about the programmes.
Someone who didn't know better might think we have a normal

relationship. Not good, but at least approaching normal.

But, like I said, I was glad when she was out of the house. I did a lot of thinking then. In fact, that was basically all I did for a couple of weeks. Do you know something? In all the time Mum and I spent chatting, Kiffo's name wasn't mentioned once. Not once. Isn't that something? Isn't that remarkable? But even though his name was never mentioned, he was always in my head. I think he always will be. And I suppose you want to know more about that. My feelings now that Kiffo is gone. How I'm coping with the knowledge that I'll never see his red hair again, or hear his voice, or laugh at his treatment of a relief teacher. That kind of stuff. Well, I'm sorry, but I don't want to talk about it. If you don't know how I'm thinking and feeling, then you've either not read this book carefully enough, or I've not done a very good job writing it. And I'm not arrogant enough to think it might not be the latter. Whatever, I don't want to say anything else. Even writers have to keep some things private, don't they?

A writer. That's what I am now. This book is proof of that, don't you think? I'm not saying what kind of a writer, mind you. But a writer – I guess I can say at least that about myself. This book was written in those six weeks. What's more, I really enjoyed writing it. There were so many times when I felt completely lost in it, so that hours and hours would go by and I wouldn't be aware of it. Sometimes Mum would leave for work in the morning and then be home about five minutes later, or so it would seem. And I'd have filled pages and pages, without being aware that I'd filled them. A bit scary in a way.

And at some stage in the writing – I don't know when, I'm not even sure that there was a specific moment – I made up my mind to go back to school. There was a time there, you see, when I didn't think I could face it. After everything that had happened, I thought it might have been easier to avoid all the problems associated with school. Maybe get a job for a while and then do a bit of travelling before I finished my education. But I know now that I really enjoy writing, that I want to make a career of it, if I'm good enough. And I don't want to wait. So that means doing English in senior school. Learning more about Shakespeare and sonnets and all that kind of thing. Getting some idea of what real writers are like and how they go about the whole business. I know that I'll probably be doing a lot of essay writing, which isn't the stuff I've got into over the last six weeks. But it's all writing. And there is something exciting about having a blank page in front of you and filling it with not just words, but the right words, in the right order. Yeah, I know. I'm a bit odd. I suppose I'll have to be happy with being odd. To be honest, I think I always was happy with it. Maybe it just took Kiffo to make me realise it.

I guess you weren't expecting a happy ending, not after everything that happened. A good job, too. Here I am, alienated from school with a mother who's barking mad and not even one good friend to share things with. So a not unhappy ending is perhaps the best we can hope for. So here it is.

While I was writing everything down, I came to a few conclusions about what went on between me, Kiffo and the Pit Bull. Isn't it strange? You can be there, living a life, but not fully aware of what it all means. Writing has given me a different perspective on events. Homophones, for example. I never realised how important homophones could be. Or the power of the Internet. Or the power of perseverance. I explained all of these things to that police officer, the one with the shifted face. Remember her? I went to see her at the police station just before I wrote this chapter. Turns out her name is Alyce Watson. Constable Alyce Watson. And do you know something? She's really nice. And clever.

So, are you totally confused now? Don't be. It makes perfect sense. You just need to look at it from a different angle.

Harrison paced the carpet, puffing away on her meerschaum pipe. I knew the signs of old. My friend was onto something and the game was afoot. I knew better than to interrupt her train of thought, however. If I knew one thing about Harrison it was that she would reveal the products of her singular mind when the time suited her, when all the pieces had fallen into place. I pretended to read a report that lay on my desk. Not five minutes went past before Harrison stopped pacing and seated herself in the old horsehair chair in the corner.

'Homophones, Constable Watson,' she said. 'A much underrated linguistic phenomenon, don't you think?'

I glanced up at Harrison. There was a bright gleam in her eye and I knew that whatever she had been considering, in that remarkable brain everything had fallen into place.

'Homophones, old girl?' I replied. 'I'm not sure I understand.'

Harrison took the pipe from her lips.

'Indeed, Watson! You should really broaden your mind. I am, of course, referring to words that have identical phonological characteristics but widely differing semantic qualities.'

Harrison could see that I was no wiser, so she put it into layperson's language.

'Words that sound the same, but have different meanings! Like "bough", the branch of a tree, and "bow", the act of bending at the waist. Or "waist", the expanding flesh between your ribs and your hips, Watson, and "waste", what time is going to, while I am engaged in explaining the obvious! Homophones.'

'Steady on, old girl,' I remonstrated. 'I know what you mean, but I'm afraid I don't see what it has to do with the case.'

Harrison sprang to her feet and resumed pacing.

'It has everything to do with the case, my dear Watson. Everything. Let me explain. You remember my meeting with Jonno, the tattooed scallywag employed by Kiffo to trace the movements of my arch enemy, the Pit Bull?'

'Indeed I do, Harrison.'

'Then you may remember that at one point in the conversation, Jonno said, "And the address of this pain?" '

Once again I was amazed at Harrison's prodigious memory.

'Words to that effect, Harrison.'

'No, Watson. Not "to that effect". They were the exact words. But my point Watson, is that one might reasonably assume that "pain" was being used in that colloquial manner that some chaps employ when they are referring to people who are an inconvenience. A "pain in the arse", I believe. But what if Jonno was actually saying, "And the address of this Payne?" P-A-Y-N-E.'

'Good Lord, Harrison,' I exclaimed. 'The real

name of the Pit Bull! But hold on a moment, old girl. So what if he was saying "Payne"? I can't see how that would be significant.'

'My dear fellow, Jonno should not have known her name. He expressed an ignorance of her very existence. Neither Kiffo nor myself revealed any such information, yet Jonno, it seems, knew her name.'

My head was swimming, but I felt that something was not quite right. Finally, I spotted the flaw.

'Perhaps Jonno did say "pain". P-A-I-N. Maybe you're looking for a homophone where one doesn't exist, my dear Harrison!'

'Indeed, Watson. The thought had occurred to me. Yet as I was writing the sentence, from my recollections of our meeting, it struck me as wrong somehow. It jarred. I have, as you know, an encyclopedic knowledge of contemporary slang and I feel certain that this particular phrase is not one that would have occurred to someone like Jonno. It is too middle-class, hardly "colourful" enough for someone of his social background. No, the more I thought about it, the more I was convinced that Jonno did indeed know the Pit Bull and that he was keen to keep this information from us. I was then

forced to think about his motivation. What if Jonno was working for the Pit Bull? He is, as we know, a small-time figure in the criminal underworld. What if he alerted the Pit Bull to the fact that Kiffo and I were on her trail? What if, as a result of this information, the Pit Bull decided to arrange the untimely death of Kiffo? And myself?'

'Good Lord, Harrison!' I exclaimed, leaping to my feet. 'It fits. But proof, my dear girl. Where is the proof?'

Harrison puffed on the pipe, and a foul cloud of acrid smoke curled up to the ceiling.

'I needed to clarify the links between the Pit Bull, Jonno and the Kiffings. The Pit Bull asserted that she had had dealings with a member of Kiffo's family, presumably in her capacity as a drug counsellor. And I do recall seeing that family member in the company of the aforesaid Jonno some years ago. Kiffo confirmed that the Pit Bull had had contact with his family in the past, contact that he did not like or trust. However, he was very protective and may have resented the kind of professional help that she was offering. So, as I said, the connections were there, but something didn't ring true. Consequently, I did some more checking. It transpires *that the Pit Bull did not receive her counsellor qualification until three years ago, a full year after the tragic demise of the Kiffing family member. Why would she have had dealings with that person, if she was not a qualified counsellor? This leaves us with the intriguing notion that, rather than counselling him on his addiction, she was possibly encouraging it!'*

'Dash it all, Harrison,' I said. 'I'm sure you are right. When have you not been right? But we still don't have proof of a link between Jonno and the Pit Bull!'

Harrison took the pipe from her mouth and reached down into the pocket of her tweed jacket. She produced two photographs and handed them to me.

'There is a local casuarina tree with which I am familiar, Watson. I spent many hours under its gentle boughs recently. Fortunately, I took with me my trusty Canon compact camera. The two photographs you have in your hand are evidence that our tattooed scallywag has made visits to the Pit Bull's house. Long visits, Watson. Now I know that this could be explained away. Jonno is, after all, the kind of person who might want to avail himself of the Pit Bull's professional expertise, if

he indeed suffers from an addiction to narcotics. But why go to her house? That would, I feel, be unlikely. It does not seem consistent with professional practice.'

As always, I was amazed by Harrison's ability to make connections. I could only gaze in awe as she continued, unperturbed by my thunderstruck expression.

'And, finally, my dear Watson, there is the strange business with the naltrexone. If you remember, Kiffo and I saw her receive a bag of white powder from the Ferret, a bag that she asserted contained naltrexone, a drug used in the treatment of heroin addiction. Yet it is a matter of public record, Watson, and one that can be verified easily through the World Wide Web, that naltrexone is generally prescribed in fifty-milligram tablets to be taken orally. There would be no reason to grind those tablets down to a powder. In fact, it would make the administering of the drug much more difficult. Which leads me to conclude that it wasn't naltrexone at all.'

I considered everything Harrison had said. It made sense. There was no hard evidence, of course, but I knew that it was only a matter of time before she produced it. There was only one thing I could say.

'*Brilliant, Harrison.*'

'*Elementary, Constable Watson.*'

Actually, she didn't say 'brilliant'. But she was interested. She took the photographs from me. And she took loads of notes. She said that she would have a word with a couple of her colleagues and that she'd keep me informed. I think she will, too. I can generally tell when I'm being fed bullshit, and she didn't give me that impression.

Oh, she also warned me to leave it with her now. Not to go back to the Pit Bull's house, or anything. Maybe she was worried about my safety. Then again, perhaps she was conscious of the whole stalking issue. I can't tell. It seemed like excellent advice to me, whichever way you looked at it.

Trouble is, I never have been good at following advice. It's one of the many things that me and Kiffo had in common.

PRESENT DAY.

You pick up a sheaf of papers from the printer, and a sigh of satisfaction escapes your lips. It is done. Finished. You raise your head from your desk and look at a photograph hanging on the wall in front of you. It is a photograph of a red-haired boy and a flat-chested girl with glasses. They are leaning casually against the school railings. They look happy together. You smile even as you feel a hard lump of pain in your chest.

'Kiffo,' you say. 'I think that in the end you'll find I kept my promise.'

Chapter 26
Connected

'Hello. You have reached the home of Calma and the Fridge. We can't come to the phone right now because, frankly, we suspect that you want to sell us Life Insurance, an investment opportunity on the Gold Coast or solar heating for a pool we don't own. If that isn't your intention, please leave your name and number after the beep and we'll get back to you. Or not, as the case may be . . .'

'. . . Calma Harrison? Alyce Watson. Hi. Listen, there have been a number of developments regarding the matter you brought to our attention and I think you'll find them . . . interesting. We will need a formal statement from you. Could you please call to arrange a time to come in? Speak to you soon, Calma. Bye.'

Dear Calma,

A charming and sophisticated gentleman at the pub last night kindly attempted to re-adjust my underwear for me. Not realising that he had only my personal comfort in mind, I punched him in the face and catapulted his false teeth into another customer's steak and chips. As a result, my employment has, by mutual agreement, been terminated.

I can't say I'm disappointed. Reluctantly, I am starting to think that, despite your many and obvious faults, you might have a point about my work ethic. Fancy discussing this, and other issues, over a toothless steak and chips tonight? My treat.

Love,
The Fridge

Dear Fridge,

It's amazing what a change of rubber seals and a quick defrost will do to your efficient running. I think I can fit you in to my busy schedule, particularly since I am keen to hear all the sordid details of your last day at work.

Love,

Calma

P.S. Incidentally, do you think there might be a market for steak fillets that chew themselves?

ASSIGNMENT:

Write a description of a place, person or thing in such a way that you demonstrate an understanding of the use of similes.

RESPONSE:

Student's name: *Jaryd Kiffing*
Subject: *Calma Harrison*

Calma is like a girl that I know. She's like, you know, smart and everything but she's also like the best mate that anyone could have. She's never talked to me like I'm dumb. I like her, like loads. I trust her like I don't trust no one else.

END OF SEMESTER REPORT:

Student's name: *Jaryd Kiffing*
Teacher: *Ms Brinkin*
Subject: *English*
Grade: *E*
Attitude: *E*

<u>Comments:</u>
Jaryd has completely wasted his time this semester. He has been resistant to learning and disruptive in class. His written work shows little understanding, insight or sensitivity.

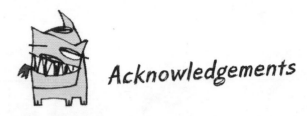

Acknowledgements

There are two things that all writers need: encouragement and then more encouragement. I have been fortunate that so many people have supplied these unstintingly. Thanks to my family, local and distant, for their support. Kris and Kari, you always believed. Lauren and Brendan, thanks for reading the manuscript and providing important insights (and for water-throwing, Lauren!) My gratitude, also, to Peter Styles for checking certain parts of the narrative. Jodie Webster and Erica Wagner, of Allen & Unwin, took a raw manuscript and transformed it. This book could not have been written without their expertise and belief. I would also like to thank Penni Russon for her intelligent and sensitive assessment of the first draft, and Leah Thaxton for her enthusiasm and skill in preparing the UK edition.

Above all else, my wife, Nita, was a reader, critic and guide, and an unfailing support when things got tough. It is impossible to adequately acknowledge her influence and contribution. Beggar that I am, I am poor even in thanks.